INSATIABLE

INSATIABLE

RHYS EVERLY

HeartEyes Press

LOGAN

As the plane descends, the green mountains of Vermont greet me in all their grace, and a warmth takes over my body.

I can feel the change coming and I can't fucking wait for it.

I can't wait to see what kind of men Vermont's got to offer. To find out if the guys around here can scream my name just as loud, and with just as much indulgence, as all the other guys across the world.

My dick throbs at the mere prospect of some fresh arse. At the promise of that sweet American accent escaping guys' lips, begging me for more. At the thought of wrapping someone, anyone, around my finger for a night or two and adding them to my little black book.

I step out of the plane and look at the blue sky above me, taking a deep breath. Yeah, it smells like maple syrup and sex here. I should do just fine.

I walk into Burlington International and go through passport control before I come up to the main lounge and locate the car rental kiosk.

The guy behind the counter is a palatable young man with cropped dark hair, blue eyes, and a clean-shaven face. He's dressed in a white shirt and black tie, and boy, oh boy, I may have to start my "research" early.

I mean, who in my place wouldn't love this sinful young man on his knees, his tie tight around his throat and in my hands while he sucks me to my heart's content?

"Hello, sir," he says. "Can I help you?"

I lean on the counter, and I know my muscles flex under the woolen pine-green jumper I'm wearing because he glances at my arm before he looks me straight in the eyes.

Yes. Definitely a palatable young man. Maybe I should slip him my card. Or maybe I can wait around for his break so we can go at it in the airport restrooms.

"I...booked a car," I say, and by the way he catches his breath and bites his lip, I can tell he loves my accent.

"S-sure. What's the name?" he asks.

This should be fun. Let's see if he passes the test.

"Graves. Logan Graves," I tell him.

His eyes shoot wide open for a second before he covers it up by nodding. But I catch it. The glint of recognition. The processing of my name in his head. He types something on a keyboard in front of him, and when he looks up at me, it's all but an invitation to kiss those lips.

"Let me get your key for you," he says, sauntering away from me to the wall behind him. When he gets to the door that's there, his hand lingers on the handle for a moment before opening it.

"I can...help you search for it," I tell him, deepening my voice, letting the suggestion pour out of me.

The guy turns around and gives me a suggestive grin that's already getting me hard and revving, and I have to fight the beast inside me. Fight the urge to jump over the counter and take him right here, right now.

"Sure you can," he says in an equally suggestive tone, so I

walk around the counter and into the back room, where I proceed to get his lips around my cock and make my fantasy a reality.

Fifteen minutes later, I'm in my rental and on my way to Burlington, ready to move on to my next conquest.

It's been a while since I've been to this side of the Atlantic. And even the last couple of times I was stateside, it was in the hustle and bustle of New York or San Francisco. I've never been to small town Americana, but taking in the scenery, the big houses, the quiet streets, the wide space, my whole body feels ready for the All-American boy experience.

It only takes me ten minutes to find Church Street and the flat address of my online vacation rental.

I knock on the door and wait, trying to picture the owner and whether I'm going to get lucky for a second time today.

When the door opens, I get my answer.

"Hi! You must be Logan," the woman says.

As far as women go, she's beautiful. Long chestnut-colored waves, a pretty smile, and a decent-size chest. I also notice her curvy body and wide hips. Not that I'm attracted to her. I learned pretty early in life that girls don't do it for me. Not by a long shot.

"You…you can't be Steve," I say.

I want to double-check my listing because I'm pretty sure I'm supposed to be meeting a guy.

"Oh yeah, my husband had an errand to run, but I hope I'm good enough," she says with a chuckle and steps aside, inviting me in. "I'm Lorelai."

"Pleasure to meet you," I tell her, giving her my cheekiest of smiles.

I take her hand in mine and kiss the back of it. As expected, she all but swoons. Just because she's not my cup of tea, doesn't mean I don't know how to charm a lady.

"Oh man. I knew you'd be a gentleman," she tells me.

"Thank you. I try."

Everywhere but in the bedroom, of course.

She dismisses my attempt at modesty with a wave of her hand.

"Look at you being all British. The girls around town will be lining up to catch a piece of you." She grins.

"And what about the boys?" I ask. "Will there be boys lining up?"

She takes a moment's pause before she gives me another smile and a wave.

"Those, too, if you like. Trust me. Everyone goes wild for that sexy British accent. And it doesn't hurt you're a bit of a silver-fox."

Don't I know *that* already? I've been to enough places around the world to know that I'm a hot piece of ass wherever I go.

"Oh, Lorelai. You're going to make me blush," I tell her.

"Just telling the truth," she says as she turns. "Why don't I show you around? I'm sure you've had a long, tiresome trip."

I shrug but don't comment. I spend most of my life in planes, when not in bedrooms, that I barely ever get jet lagged.

Lorelai takes me around the flat. It's quite the cozy space, with red-bricked walls and large arched windows that let all the sunlight in, washing the living room in warm colors.

There's a TV in between two of them and a sofa opposite. A coffee table with magazines fanned out sits on top of a fluffy red rug.

Then there's the kitchen on the other side, small but functional, with white cupboards and a polished birch counter that boasts a coffee maker, a toaster, and microwave all in matching ivory.

The bedroom is a little more plain, with the bare minimum

of furniture, but a large green painting on the wall takes up most of the space over the king-size bed.

"I hope you like the apartment," she says when we come back to the living room.

"It's great, thanks."

It will do just fine for what I need.

"You're *very* welcome," she replies. "So…what brings you to Vermont?"

"I thought I'd take in the scenery and catch up with an old friend."

Of course my plans are far more aspirational, but she doesn't need to know that.

"Oh, anyone I might know?"

"You might, actually. He's got a bookstore right down the street. Harrison Fletcher?"

Her smile widens.

"Of course I do. There's hardly anyone around Church Street who doesn't. Any plans while you're here?"

"Well," I tell her. "The plan is to finish my book, but we'll see how that goes."

The moment I mention my book, she clasps her hands together and swoons.

"Oh my. You're a writer?"

"That I am."

"That's so exciting. I've always admired people who can write books. I don't know how you do it. Coming up with an entire made-up story like that," she says.

"My books aren't entirely fictional." I smirk.

"You're published?" she asks, and I nod. "Anything I might have read?"

I laugh and take my jacket off, leaning against the back of the sofa.

"Maybe," I tell her. "Do you read…erotica?"

Her hands stay wound together on her chest, but her face reddens as she grins.

"Occasionally," she says. "I mainly read mysteries. But I'll definitely check your books out if you tell me your pen name."

I laugh again and take a card out of my back pocket.

"No pen name. Just my real one," I say as I hand it to her. "And warning, my books are extremely saucy. Not for the faint of heart."

Lorelai grabs the card and reads it before she turns to me, interest piqued, and fans herself with the tiny piece of paper.

"Now I know what I'm doing with my evening," she says.

"Evening?" I ask and look outside the window, realizing I have lost track of time. I put my hand in my pocket again and take the pocket watch that's always there, its gold metal case cool to the touch, and I clasp it open to check the time.

It's still in London time, so I move the hands five hours back.

"That's rather unusual," she says, looking down at my pocket watch.

"Oh yeah," I say and close it in my hands. "I happened upon this auction, and I just...had to have it."

Of course, she doesn't need to know I happened upon that auction because of a sexy millionaire I was pursuing. She can find out if she reads my book, *The Millionaire that Sucked*.

"It's gorgeous," Lorelai says and drops her hands to her sides, straightening her back. "Well. You probably have lots to do, so I won't keep you. I've left my and my husband's number in the kitchen, so if you find you're missing something or want a tour guide, give us a call."

"Thank you. I'm sure I'll be fine," I tell her, and she leaves.

Before I do anything else, I get undressed and take a shower to get the trip off my body then put on a fresh pair of clothes, ready to seize my evening.

The whole point of being here is to refill my creative well so I can finish my work-in-progress and get it out of the way.

And what better way than tasting some of the local flavor.

As I'm putting my shoes on, my phone pings, and I pick it up thinking it's another mobile network message about tariff charges and roaming.

Instead, I find an email from my agent.

From: Chloe Thompson
Subject: Deadline
Hi Logan,
How's Vermont? I hope you got there alright. I've spoken to Janet, and she wants an update on your manuscript.
Can you please let me know how far along you are with the WIP so I can let her know?
Best,
Chloe.

I read and reread the email so many times the words start to blur.

Here it is again. The dreaded email. The dreaded update request. The bloody "I have nothing, and I probably won't have anything, no matter how many extensions I'm given" update.

Hopefully, the Green Mountain State will reinvigorate me. I mean, it's not like I've lost all passion for my work. I still like the research part. The going-out and having wild, steamy adventures part. That is a piece of me that can't—won't—ever die down. It's the writing part of said adventures that I can't do anymore.

And of course now I'm going back to my browser and reading the reviews of *Claiming the Italian Gigolo* like I find myself doing so much more lately, every time I think about the looming deadline.

My readers didn't just hate my last release, they absolutely annihilated me.

Boring.

Same old shit.

Bloody dreadful.

Logan is getting old and it shows.

When will bedding every walking thing get trendy again? When Graves stops writing.

And those are just the tame ones. I scroll and scroll through the hundreds of reviews, wondering where I went wrong and how it was missed by my agent, editor, proofreader, and all the professional readers. Is my publisher trying to stay in my good graces because of the ludicrous money I've made them? Or have they started losing their grip on the industry? Is my writing all that shit? When did it all turn around?

Suddenly the walls are closing in, and I can't believe I've taken a trip across the ocean and this...all of this...failure has followed me here.

I close the tab on my browser. I lock my phone and put it away in my jacket.

No.

No more self-induced paralysis. Not tonight. This trip is my chance to refuel and find that passion I lost somewhere along the way, and I'll be damned if I let the fear take over on day one.

Not yet. Not before I at least fucking try. Not before I've

had the chance to fuck some men and let our encounters inspire new stories.

So that's exactly what I do. I go out and have some fun. And I hook up with not one, but two beauties. Twinks that swoon over me the moment I introduce myself and explain what I do. And I take them back to my flat with a couple of bottles of wine, where I have them in turn, both eager to be a character in my next book. To be a Logan Graves' conquest. And in the shuffle of the night and the joy, I forget all about the email and the reviews and the fact my career might be over.

The sun blasts my eyes the next morning and rudely awakens me, although the twinks in my bed stay asleep.

I unearth myself from the tangle of legs and arms and get out of bed, trotting naked to the kitchen and getting the coffee machine running straight away. Then I jump into the shower, and by the time I come out, the twinks are on the sofa, cups in hand, drinking my coffee, just as naked as when they were in bed.

"Good morning," one of them says.

I can't remember their names, and I'm not bothered to ask. What I care about is the fact they're loitering.

"Morning. You want to use the shower?" I urge more than tell them.

"You should have told us you were going in. We could have joined you," the same guy says.

When I go to the coffee machine, the pot is almost empty, and I have to take a deep breath before I turn around.

"I need to go soon, so if you wouldn't mind," I tell them.

The guys look at each other and put their cups down. Then they go to the bathroom, and just before they close the door, one of them drapes himself over it and looks at me with a sexy pout.

"You're more than welcome to join *us*," he says.

"I'm all right, thanks," I tell him and lift my empty cup in a salute.

He seems to get the message and closes the door, so I get busy making another pot of coffee so when they finally come out, I've got my own brew in hand.

"How long are you in town for?" says one of them.

"Not long," I lie as I grab my laptop and sit at the dining table.

"I thought you had to go out," says the other.

"I do," I reply without looking at him.

"Oh, are you going to write about us? Did you get a stroke of inspiration? Can we read it after you're done?" says the first guy. Or is it the same guy?

I don't know. And frankly, I'm so over them already. Way too clingy. No one likes a clinger.

"Don't forget anything on your way out," I tell them and open my emails to reply to Chloe.

I offer her another lie, of course, but it's necessary. Once it's sent, I look over my open manuscript window, the cursor blinking in the empty page, and think about last night's encounter.

It has been a long time since I wrote a ménage. Maybe that can be the subject of the next book.

"Ass," says one of them as he opens the front door, all dressed now, and walks out.

His friend, right behind him, gives me an awkward smile and follows until I'm finally left in peace again.

"He was such a gentleman last night." I hear them talking outside. "Should have known it was all an act."

I try to ignore it. I try to forget it. But when I leave the flat half an hour later, it follows me all the way outside.

Am I really such a failure that even the guys I sleep with don't like me anymore? Or am I acting like a pig and don't even realize?

Isn't it standard for a one-night stand to leave in the morning without a word? Had I not made it clear to them that was all it was?

"Sir Graves!" Harrison shouts across the bar when I step into his establishment, Vino and Veritas.

"Fletcher," I smile and approach him.

He's standing next to a guy who's sitting in front of a laptop at the bar, with a mountain of paperwork next to him.

I give my old friend a hug before he introduces me to Tanner, the bar manager.

"Hey," Tanner replies, with an unreadable face that I immediately want to decipher. "Nice to meet you."

"You too, gorgeous," I tell him, only for Harrison to drag me away from him.

"I know what you're thinking, and I can tell you already. Don't!" He laughs, but I can also tell he's being serious.

I put my hands up in surrender.

"Fine. I'll find another toy to play with."

He rolls his eyes, but I ignore it. No one said I'm easy to deal with. He can't be blamed for being so protective of his friend.

"Anyway…when did you get here?" Harrison asks.

"Yesterday afternoon."

"You should have called. We could have gone for dinner."

I wave him off.

"Nonsense. You've got your beau to entertain, and I can entertain myself."

"No doubt about that." He laughs. "Want to get a coffee next door? Catch up?"

"Sure."

"Cool. Just give me five minutes and then I'm all yours."

I turn around to look at the place. It's a cute bar. There's a stage and a few tables scattered in the middle with booths along the front. The tones are warm and the vibe quite ethereal. I can imagine it gets even more cozy in the evenings, when the lights are down and the music on.

As I take in the place, a guy walks through the door, and my breath catches.

He's got short dark hair, sideburns, a patchy beard with a hint of a moustache and soul patch, puckered pink lips, and dark eyes that give him a sinful Mediterranean scowl to die for.

He's sporting blue jeans, a denim jacket with a white woolen lapel, and a red checkered shirt.

All-American boy and Turkish delight rolled into one.

He shoots straight for the bar, and as he passes me by, offers me a glance. The deep scowl and his sad eyes give me pause.

Jeez. Is everyone a grump around here?

But then I see a twinkle in his eye as he paints a fake smile on his face and approaches Tanner, and I decide.

He, whoever he is, will be my next conquest.

BRODY

When I wake up, I instinctively turn around and drape my hand over the rest of the bed, where *he* used to be.

It's been three months, and I still haven't shaken him out of my thoughts, my routine, my life.

He still haunts me everywhere I go. His memory around my house. The feel of his body against mine under the covers. The mouthwatering scents of his cooking.

Fucking Theo.

I don't know what more kick I need to boot him out of the permanent space he takes up in my head. What other reason does one need than being left at the altar in front of family and friends, waiting on my big fucking day. I should have known something like that would happen. And yet, I didn't see the signs.

Were there even any signs? Or had he been that good an actor?

Well, considering he wasted two years of my life, I'd say even if he wasn't a good actor, I was certainly a bad judge of character.

But then again, you don't go about in life thinking your lover, the person you spend all your time with and who you adore more than anything in the world, will dupe you so bad.

"It's your own damn fault, Mercier," I tell my reflection in the mirror because he deserves to hear it.

Over and over and over again. Until I get it through my stupid noggin and shake off his ghost from what's supposed to be my home.

"Today is a brand-new day," I say. I've been doing this a lot since Theo dumped me. Talking to myself. I had become so used to having someone to talk to in my life, that I can't stand the silence inside these four walls.

After I shower and dress, I go into the kitchen and whip up a fresh batch of pancakes for breakfast, using a generous amount of my maple wine over them. Nothing says good morning like booze and sugar, after all.

The sweet, smoky fermented syrup awakens my senses, And whatever complaint my stomach might have about such a strong aperitif, I drown with pancakes and coffee.

"It's a good batch," I say to the room. "Although maybe it needs a bit more smokiness to it."

And with that, I go up to my fridge, pick up a business card stuck to it with a magnet, and call the whiskey distillery I work with from time to time.

I order a used cask and then retreat to the back of my house, through the little hallway and the door at the end, into my own sugarhouse-slash-distillery.

I get a fresh batch of maple wine distilled and bottled and stick the labels on each bottle individually, letting Tina roll on the river through the speakers.

It helps time pass faster, and the mundane job of picking a sticker off and applying it perfectly on each bottle easier.

When I'm done it's ten in the morning, and I know I have to start doing my rounds. So I take the crate I've just prepared and stack it at the other end of the distillery where all the other crates are sitting, waiting to be sold.

"Don't worry, my babies. I'll find you a home soon enough," I tell them, tapping one of the dozen crates on my way out.

"Good morning, honey," I say as soon as I get into my pickup and smooth my hands along the wheel. "Ready for another day of begging?"

I turn the ignition, and she responds with a roaring rev.

"Yeah. Me too, sweetheart," I say and set off toward Burlington for my least favorite part of this job.

"Well, you're your own boss, Mercier. Hire someone to do it," I tell the guy in my rearview mirror.

"I can't afford it. If only I could afford it."

And that's pretty much how my journey to the city goes. Me arguing with myself. Because no one said sugarmakers aren't crazy.

"It's Theo's fault," I say. "If he'd just put up with his midlife crisis, we'd be married now, and I wouldn't be going cuckoo out here on my own."

And since my mind works in mysterious ways, I decide to scream the lyrics of "Out Here On My Own" at the top of my lungs.

A car overtakes me, and I feel the stare of its driver at my window. So I match his stare and raise him a frown.

Seconds later, the guy has overtaken me, and I'm free to go back to butchering my song.

It's my car, my right, damn it!

When I get to town, I park and go on my rounds. Most restaurants will be opening soon, and most bars will be getting their deliveries in at this time, so it's the perfect opportunity for some pestering.

Perfect being a subjective word, of course. There's nothing perfect about begging people to buy your shit.

My first stop is Bistro Charme. The bar manager is standing at the host stand going through a floor plan—probably organizing their reservations for today.

"Hi. Oh, we're not open just yet, but if you hold on minute, I can get you a table," he says, looking right at me.

I stand in front of him and my eyes tighten. That's a new low.

"Jordan? It's me. Brody. Mercier," I snap. "We went to school together?"

Recognition flashes across his eyes, and he shakes his head.

"Of course. Brody. Sorry," he says. "How are you?"

"I'm good, thanks." I can't help it if my voice comes out flat and frustrated. I *am* frustrated. I'm forgettable too, apparently.

"What can I do for you?"

I put my hands in the pockets of my denim jacket and shrug.

"Just wondering if you need to place any more orders for Mercier's Wine," I tell him.

His eyes spark again, as if he only just remembered who I am.

"Oh, Mercier's Wine. Yeah. I just counted my inventory, and I still have the three bottles we ordered last month," he says.

"You ordered those two months ago. And one was a sample." I meant to be nice about it. I meant to tell him that one was a gift for him to try. Something to enjoy with his family and friends so he can then go on and sell the other two, but instead it comes out wrong.

Everything comes out of my mouth wrong lately.

"I don't know what to tell you, buddy," Jordan says, and I shake my head involuntarily.

"Let me know when you do," I tell him and spin around to walk out before he can add insult to injury.

I take a deep breath.

"Not today, Satan," I say to soothe myself, looking up at the sky, and head for my next stop.

And I keep repeating it after every establishment I visit.

Naturally, no one needs any more supply. No one even remembers me. Even though I make a habit every other week of going in and checking on them. I could do it from home. Call them up and ask them. But they say this face-to-face stuff is more personal or some shit.

Whoever came up with it, didn't know what they were talking about.

As I come out of the fourth place, my phone rings and I answer.

"Hi, Mom."

I don't even need to check the screen. I know it's her. It's midday, and that's her call time. Not that anyone else ever calls me.

"Sweetie! How are you?" She's practically screaming through the connection.

"I'm fine, Mom," I tell her.

"You don't sound fine."

I sigh.

"Mom, we can't keep having the same conversation every. Single. Day," I say.

"Well, I'm hoping one of these days you'll actually come up with a different answer."

"Right."

"You can't blame me for trying. We're worried about you," she says.

"Harper, leave the kid alone," Dad says in the distance.

"Listen to your husband, Harper," I agree with him.

"Oh shush, both of you. Do you have to be so much like your father?"

"What? Witty, strong, and handsome?" I ask.

"Pig-headed, grumpy, and irritable," she answers.

"Gotta go now, Mom."

This conversation is *not* helping my current situation.

"Promise me you're coming for dinner tonight," she says.

"We'll see."

"Promise!"

"Mom!" I raise my voice, scaring a girl walking past me.

"If you don't come over, we'll come to you," she says in that singsong muffled tone that tells me not to take her threat lightly.

"Fine. I'll be there at six," I tell her, hanging up before she can complain about that being too late.

I have a job to do.

My next stop is Vino and Veritas. I really need to get rid of at least one crate today. Otherwise I'll be running out of space very soon. And more importantly, I'll become exactly what Theo said I was in his letter to me. The one he gave to his best man to deliver to me right at the altar.

Oh the magical time that was my wedding day.

"More like doomsday," I mutter to myself and go through the main double doors, turning left to enter the bar side of the establishment.

Tanner, the bar manager, is sitting at the bar on a laptop, his back turned to me while chatting to Harrison. There's a stranger standing nearby, and he stares at me as I walk up to Tanner, but I ignore him.

Even though he's got salt-and-pepper hair, ice-blue eyes, and a gorgeous beard I'd love to run my hands over. Even though he's a mountain of a man. He's several inches taller than me and buff as hell underneath the tight, gray sweatshirt he's wearing.

I'm not tempted by him. No siree. I'm done with gorgeous men. Or men, full stop. And I'm certainly done with letting handsome men dictate my life and the wild thoughts in my head.

Nobody's got time for that crap.

"Tanner!" I say as I approach both men at the bar.

Harrison turns around first and smiles, greeting me by name. At least there's someone around here that remembers me. You'd think this town suffers from a collective amnesia or something ever since my relationship fell apart.

"Oh, hey, Brody," Tanner says.

I stand there, hands in pockets, and wait. I can feel eyes on my back, but whatever urge I have to turn around, I stomp it down.

"Any news? Tell me you have news," I say to Tanner.

Tanner grimaces and scratches the back of his head.

"Sorry, dude4. It's still not selling."

I try not to let the puff of air that escapes me show, or my shoulders hunch. How successful I am, I cannot know without looking in the mirror.

That's the thing with me lately. I can't feel my muscles, can't control my face, which seems frozen in a perma-frown; I have no control over my body. Everything is numb inside. And empty. So empty that sometimes I wonder if there was ever anyone in there in the first place.

"Of course not," I say. "Why would it?"

The tickle on my back becomes more intense, until I can

feel the physical heat of the silver-fox behind me, standing almost too close for comfort.

Although, the kind of proximity I'm comfortable with lately is a lot less than it used to be.

Thanks, Theo.

"I don't know what to tell you man. Maple wine is...niche. It's a tough sell," Tanner says apologetically.

Not sure why he's being apologetic. It's not his fault I'm shit at what I do. Even if I think my stuff tastes like heaven in a bottle. But what the hell do I know anymore? I used to think I knew what love was too, and look where that got me.

"Maple wine, huh? Sounds intriguing to me," the guy next to me says in a British accent that should make me weak in the knees, but it just irritates me instead.

"Don't patronize me," I tell him.

I expect him to glower at me, like people tend to do when I snap at them lately, but he grins. What kind of sick bastard is he?

"Maybe it's volume you're lacking. I can get you a crate so you can put it on display?" I say, but I've already lost hope of getting anywhere.

Why do I keep punishing myself with this crap? Maybe I should just lock myself in my house and drink my own stock till I die. Sounds more appealing than walking around begging people to give my failed ass a chance.

"I'd love to..." Tanner says, and he doesn't even need to finish his sentence for me to know what he'll say next.

"That's fine," I say. "See you. I guess."

I turn around and find the British guy staring at me as I brace myself to walk out with my pride still intact.

"What?" I ask when his gaze lingers. "Hasn't anyone taught you it's rude to stare?"

There must be something wrong with the guy. He grins even more at my reprimand. Idiot.

"I must have skipped that lesson," he says with a shrug.

I don't dignify that with a response. I just storm out and find the next place to reject me.

Rejection.

I'm good at that.

Maybe that's all I'll ever be good at.

3

LOGAN

"Wow," Tanner says, turning back to his work while Harrison comes up to me.

"Coffee?" he asks, and I nod.

"Who was that?" I ask.

"That...was Brody Mercier," he replies. "Maple wine producer."

We walk up to the front and duck inside the bookshop, where Harrison guides me to a little coffee shop section at the far end and we sit at the counter.

"For a guy that makes maple wine, he's a tad sour," I say.

"And with good reason," Harrison says just as another tall, burly guy with short brown hair comes up behind the counter and asks me what I'd like to drink. "He's not always been like that. But he was dumped. The poor thing."

"I know a lot of guys who've been dumped," I say. "They aren't all like that."

"Yeah, well, they might be if they were left waiting at the altar," Harrison says, and the barista hands him his coffee. "Thanks, Oz."

"No problem. Say, are we talking about Brody?" the barista

asks before passing me my own coffee, the cup almost looking fake in his huge hands. As it does in mine. He's actually not bad to look at. And it's been a while since I got with someone as big as me. So I turn on the sexy smirk, even though I can feel I'm not into it. I'm still thinking about the little grump that just told me off.

"Gorgeous," I say, staring at him instead of the leafy milk pattern in my cup.

The guy raises an eyebrow but doesn't respond to my advance.

"That's the one. He was just here," Harrison says.

"Oh yeah. Of course. It is Thursday after all," Oz replies.

"He was jilted? Damn," I say. Who would be such an idiot to dump *him* at the altar? What more did they want? I may not know this Brody guy from Adam, but I wouldn't mind coming home every day and tapping *that*.

Of course, I'm not marriage material, so what the hell do I know? It's been years since I've had more than a brief affair.

"Hey, Mr. Graves," Harrison says, and I shake the thoughts out of my head and turn to look at my friend. "You're drooling."

Oz and Harrison both chuckle, but I only offer them a glower in response.

"Oh. He's even copying Brody's signature look," Oz says.

"Cut it out, you two. And you? I don't even know you," I tell him with a raised eyebrow.

"Well, that's easily rectified," he says and gives me his hand. "Oz Walker. At your service."

"Logan Graves." I say, shaking his hand.

"The Logan Graves?" Oz asks.

"The one and only," Harrison replies.

"Hey!" I whine. "That's my line."

Harrison puts his hands up and laughs. "Apologies, my lord!"

"Arse," I tell him and turn to Oz. "How about that rectifying you mentioned?"

Oz laughs and shakes his head.

"Do you hit on all the guys you meet?" he asks.

"Yup," Harrison answers for me, raising his hand.

Oz shakes his head and turns around to clean the nozzle of the milk steamer on the coffee machine.

"Does that mean you're here to conquer Vermont for your next book?" he asks, craning his neck to look at me.

Book? What book? There isn't even a chapter, let alone a book.

"Maybe. Maybe," I finally say when I put my cup back down.

"And? Have you found the object of your 'affection' yet?" Harrison asks. "Current company excluded, of course."

I shrug and turn around, taking in the bookshop, but someone outside catches my attention, coming out of a restaurant across the street.

Brody Mercier. I'd love to see him sprawled out in my bed, hanging onto my lips as if they are sweeter than maple, and have him shout out my name as I take him six ways to Sunday, effectively turning that frown upside down.

"I think I have," I say, looking back at my friend with a smirk.

Harrison checks over his shoulder for who I'd been looking at, then turns back to me in horror.

"Oh God. No. Leave the poor man alone. He's got enough to deal with without you chasing after him," he says.

I take another sip of my coffee—delicious, by the way—and sit back on the stool.

"The way I see it, he's got a bad case of the sadsies and

could use a…smile," I say. *Or a dick in his mouth. Same difference.*

"You're an idiot."

Harrison shakes his head, and Oz grimaces.

"What? You think you can get him? Good luck with that. That man has been in a rut for three months now," he says.

"Is that a challenge?" I say, addressing both of them.

Harrison rolls his eyes and sips his coffee.

"Do you ever not…um…think with your dick?" Oz asks.

"Probably not," I say.

"I know you've had a lot of 'adventures,' but Brody Mercier isn't the type to fall under your spell. He almost got married for crying out loud," Oz says.

"All the more reason to have some fun and rebound. Hard," I say. "Hey! That could be the title of my next book. *Hard Rebound with the Sugarmaker.*"

"I still don't think Brody is a guy who will want a quickie in the restroom or a BJ behind the bushes."

"Maybe not at first."

"Maybe not ever," Oz counters.

"Wanna bet on it?" I ask, the cogs already turning in my head.

I love nothing if not a challenge, and from the sound—and look of it—Brody Mercier may just be exactly what I need to get me out of my own rut. And we can both have fun in the process. And a bestseller at the end of it.

That'll show those bloody critics.

"Bet on it?" Oz asks, hesitantly.

"Yeah. Bet. You say I can't get him, and I'm telling you that I can have him in my bed by the end of the month, if not the week."

"Gosh, I knew you based your stories on real life, but I didn't realize all you think about is sex. When was the last time you went without sex for longer than a week?" Oz asks, leaning forward, a hand under his chin, brown eyes staring right at mine.

"A week? Jeez. Does anyone go through such torture?" I ask.

Harrison lets out a surprised wow next to me, but both Oz and I ignore him.

"I'll tell you what. I'll bet you can't get him into bed, and if you lose…" Oz scratches his chin and purses his lips before he speaks again. "If you lose, you can't have sex for three months."

A knot forms in my throat, and I start coughing on the coffee dregs still in my mouth.

"What the hell? Three months? That's plain torture."

Oz stands up straight again and shrugs.

"Well, if you're scared—"

"I'm not scared," I say before he can even finish. "Why would I be? I can get him like *that*." I click my fingers, and the snap seems to give me back my confidence.

Getting guys in my bed is what I do. I never fail. The guy to resist me hasn't been born yet. And Brody Mercier is no exception. He may be a challenge, but he'll be begging for my cock before long.

"If you say so," Oz smirks. "But if you lose, you go celibate. Three months."

"Fine. I lose, I go celibate." A shudder passes over my entire body at the mere suggestion. "But if you lose, I get your respect for my skills and charm."

Oz raises an eyebrow and crosses his arms.

"That's it? That's all you want from me? Respect? I thought you were going to ask for something naughtier. You, Mr. Graves, surprise me. And…" He reaches for my hand and we shake on it. "You've got yourself a deal."

My brain is already hard at work trying to figure out all the methods I can use to make him mine. I'm also suddenly itchy for my keyboard. Am I already getting rid of my writer's block?

"You've got to tell me where he hangs out, where I can find him, everything," I tell both.

"That sounds a lot like cheating," Harrison says.

"It isn't cheating. I'm new to town. So, inexperienced in Vermont," I say with a pout.

Harrison and Oz exchange a glance and chuckle before Harrison turns around back to me.

"Well, he does have a stall at the farmer's market," he says.

"When?"

BRODY

"Wine, wine. Maple wine," I mutter under my breath as people pass by my stall like I don't even exist.

Of course they all flock to the other sugarmakers selling their ware in much more fashionable packages. Like The Maple Factory's very own donut stall. Because having a bakery on Church Street isn't enough. They have to have a stall here too. Or Maple Sky. I can't believe Skyler's got a line of people waiting to get his maple cream. Maple cream of all things. Yet, it's my maple wine that's odd.

"Maple cream. Like that doesn't sound dirty," I say to no one in particular.

An old lady stops at my stall and looks at my wine display.

"Oh, that looks interesting," she says, and then looks up at me.

"Oh, it's more than interesting," I reply, and her face sinks.

Then she walks away.

"Bye to you too," I say after her, and as I follow her with my eyes, my gaze lands back on Skyler and his horde of customers. "You can fuck off too," I mutter in his direction.

"Is that an official Vermonter welcome?" a guy appears

from my left and stands in front of me, his hands in his back pockets, oozing confidence and cockiness.

It's the guy from Vino and Veritas from earlier this week. What is he doing here? And why is that voice grating on my last nerve when he's barely spoken?

"I wouldn't say official, but pretty darn close," I tell him.

His lips pout and on a hiss, he says, "If you treat strangers like that, I'd love to see how you treat friends."

And then he smirks.

"What are you smirking at?" I say. Oops. I meant to say that in my head.

Oh well. Roll with it, Brody.

"You. If it wasn't obvious. I can try again," he says and turns his head around. Then he swivels it back at me and smirks even wider than before.

"Are you having a nervous breakdown? Do I need to call 911?" I tell him.

He finally releases his hands from his pockets and rests them on my stall. Ass. Who does he think he is to be touching *my* stall?

"You don't mess around, do you? Straight to the point," he says. "I like it."

I can give you something else to like. Like the feel of my fist on your face.

At least I say that in my head. Which gives me the opportunity to take a deep breath.

"Is there something you want?" I ask him and cross my hands in front of my chest.

His eyes slit, and he stares at me for moments that feel like hours before he drops his gaze to my product.

"Absolutely. Mercier's Wine. Sounds rough around the edges," he says and picks up a bottle.

"But it's a damn fine wine," I tell him with a raised voice.

He passes the bottle from one hand to the other and grins at me.

"That's what I'm hoping," he says.

"Are you buying that or—" I start, but what's happening behind the mountain man catches my attention and makes me freeze.

Theo walks up to Maple Sky, around the stall, and stands next to Skyler, hand on the small of his back and kissing him on the cheek.

"Hey," the guy in front of me says, but his voice barely registers.

Skyler smiles at Theo, *my Theo*, and then they both start working through the line of people.

What is *my* Theo doing with him? Since when are they even a thing? Have they always been a thing? Is that why Theo dumped me?

Or is he a rebound? And since when are we rebounding already? It's not even been three months since we were supposed to get married. And now he's rebounding? Did the two years we spent together mean nothing to him? Is he already done mourning our relationship?

"He's the one that broke it off, Mercier. Of course he's done," I growl under my breath.

"Huh?" asks the guy at my stall.

I turn to him and glare.

"Are you buying or not?"

He seems to trip over my question because he continues to stare at me.

"Sure. I'm buying," he says and passes me the bottle. "Are you okay?" he asks as I bag it up for him.

"Uh huh," I reply, and my traitor eyes turn over to Maple Sky again.

They're both chatting to their customers, laughing, hell, Skyler even touches *my* Theo's hand.

What right do they have to laugh in front of me? What right does that *himbo* have to rub himself all over my fiancé.

"Ex-fiancé," I remind myself.

Only, yet again, I forget I have a customer, who turns around and watches the happy couple too.

"Tough break-up?" he asks when he turns back around.

I give him his bag and hold my hand out.

"None of your business. Twenty-five dollars," I say.

He puts his hand in the pocket of his jacket, and I find myself again looking over at Maple Sky and the two "sweethearts." Barf!

Theo hands someone their change and kisses Skyler's cheek before he joins the footfall of the market.

And what's worse? He clocks me and heads right for my stall.

"Oh, fuck." I curse whoever's stomped on my fucking luck.

"Sorry. Sorry," my customer says and gives me a handful of bills.

"No, it's not you," I tell him.

I wonder if I can keep him here a little while longer and hopefully avoid a confrontation with Theo.

I really don't want to talk to him.

"Brody," he says as he comes up to my stall, and whatever resolve I had of giving him the brush-off, or chatting to the British dude to keep me occupied, jumps out the window and leaves me all frozen and tongue-tied.

"Brod," he repeats when I don't answer him.

He runs a hand through his dark hair and pins me with his smug, clean-shaven look that used to drive me crazy for him.

"Fiancé. Erm...Theo," I say. And I almost facepalm. *Almost.*

"How's it going? Made any sales yet?" he asks, but my body refuses to cooperate.

Why is it so hard to open my damn mouth and tell him to fuck off? I literally just did that with my customer. Who is still standing there, by the way, staring down at *my* Theo.

Damn it. Theo. It's *just* Theo now. Or, well, asshole is my preferred term for him. Or should be anyway.

"Are you okay?" Theo asks.

The customer turns to look at me, and the stress of having two sets of eyes glaring makes me even more uneasy as I fist the cash in my hand even tighter.

Why can't I open my stupid trap? What the hell is wrong with me?

You're an idiot, Mercier.

"He's fine," the customer says. "Aren't you, babe?"

"Huh?" I turn to the mountain of a man.

Did he just call me babe?

The stranger walks around the stall and puts his hand. On. My. Butt.

Good thing I can't move because I'd have slapped it away and broken a couple of his fingers.

"So...dinner tonight?" he asks me, daringly giving my ass cheek a squeeze.

Theo seems unable to look at anything other than the stranger's hand, and I seem unable to stop looking at Theo.

"Brody, what's going on?" Theo asks.

The stranger's hand comes up to my cheek—like my actual face cheek—and he rests it there for a moment before planting a kiss on my temple.

"It's okay, love. I won't let him hurt you anymore."

What is he talking about? He's not gonna let who hurt me? And why does the way he says love and the ghost of his kiss on my temple make my skin all...pimply?

"Brody? Are you having an affair?" Theo asks.

And that seems to just about do it.

"Affair would imply I'm still with someone else, and last time I checked, I was single," I shout at him, making Theo, the man with his hand on my ass, and some passersby jump.

"Exactly. *Was* single," the stranger says. "And I'd like to thank you," he says, turning to Theo. "If it weren't for you, I wouldn't have the best man in the world by my side."

Damn right, best man in the world.

Wait, what? He has me? Since when? Did I miss an episode?

"You're in a relationship?" Theo turns to me.

And I don't know what it is. If it's the shock in his voice, his attitude, or the fact he sounds so judgy when he's already found a boy-toy, but I decide enough is enough.

I don't know why this stranger is pretending to be my boyfriend, but fuck it, I'm taking advantage of it while I can.

"That's none of your damn business, Theo," I tell him. "And unless you want to get a good beating by..."

Fuck. I don't know his name. What do I do?

"My baby, I'd move along now. He's the jealous type, you know," I say and make my best attempt at giving the stranger by my side googly eyes.

The stranger smirks and raises an eyebrow.

"I also have a thing for wankers who make promises and don't know how to keep them," he turns and says to Theo.

How the hell does he know about Theo and me?

Of course. He was in Vino and Veritas yesterday. He probably heard the gossip from Harrison and Tanner, or someone else, like *everyone* in this town.

"How dare you? Who do you—?" Theo starts, and I can already see the whine building on his face.

I put up with two years of that shit, I'm not putting up with any more of it without a ring on my finger.

"Baby," I tell the complete stranger next to me and bring my hand up to his neck. We're uncomfortably close, but there's nothing I can do right now. "Don't engage him. He's just poo on my shoe compared to what we have."

I can see the stranger biting down on a laugh, but he keeps up the act. He might be an ass, too, but at least he's a trooper.

"You know you're the only one I've ever loved," I say, and then I do something very unlike me.

I kiss him. Put those smackers on his and go to town. And to his credit, he doesn't hold back. He meets my tongue with his and deepens the kiss, hand on the back of my head, towering over me. I have to grapple onto my stall to keep from falling.

My body shivers with every stroke of his tongue, and I can smell his deodorant, a spicy exotic flavor that tickles my nose. The worst part is I feel a growth at my hip, and the way he presses his body to mine, I can tell it's a big growth. My dick surely takes notice.

Everything stills around us. The people, the noise, the weather. It's like we spend days, months, years even in this position while the world is frozen all around.

And then he comes up for air and time starts to move at a normal pace again.

When I look at the other side of the counter, it's empty. Theo is gone.

In his absence, I find myself *and* my senses again and push the stranger off me.

"That was...something," he whispers, and I have to bite down on how weak his breath makes me feel.

I wipe my lips with the back of my forearm and push my other hand on his body as a barrier between us. The feel of his chiseled chest under my touch makes my dick jolt in my pants.

"That was inappropriate," I tell him.

"Oh, I beg to differ. It was just what I needed."

"You're a creep. Has anyone told you that before?" I tell him, still unable to remove my hand from his chest. It feels so damn good there.

"Plenty of guys," he smirks.

"It's not a compliment," I say.

He shrugs and puts his hands in his pockets, looking down at my hand on his chest.

"That's because you don't know who I am," he says.

I finally stop touching him and cradle my hand with my other one as if it had been on fire.

"That's right. I don't know who you are. And you shouldn't have done that," I say.

"Which part? The saving you part or kissing you part?" He smirks.

And there is that smugness I saw a few minutes ago, before Theo came and put everything through the blender.

"Both," I tell him. "I don't need saving. Or kissing."

"You started the kissing, remember?"

Damn. He's right. I can't exactly play it all high-and-mighty when I went along with everything and took advantage.

"Well...in that case, thank you for your services, but I won't be needing you any longer."

"Once again...I beg to differ," the guy says, but he takes a step back. "Nice to kiss ya, Brody boy. We shall do that again soon."

"No, we shan't," I reply, but he doesn't look fazed by me.

He grins, wrinkles his lips, and turns away. And I watch him walk away, knowing it will take lots of mouthwash before I can get rid of the taste of him in my mouth.

5

LOGAN

Is it weird that I can't get that kiss out of my mind all day? From the moment I walk away until the moment I hit my pillow, it's all I can think about.

The taste of his mouth on mine, sweet and fortified, the smell of smoky molasses on him, his body pinned to mine...

It drives me so mad, I end up a walking hard-on. I've never felt like this before, and I've been with some pretty hot guys in my life.

I don't know what it is about Brody Mercier, but I'm obsessed.

Which is why, when my thoughts stray to him late at night, I slide my hand down to my cock and appease the hardness by wanking it off, bringing our kiss front and center in my mind.

The way he resisted me but still wanted to get back at the other guy. The way his tongue tried to escape mine but ended up in a tangled mess instead. The feel of my hard-on on his hips and the fullness of his butt cheek in my hand.

I spill my seed all over my stomach and hand, and even though I'm undone, I keep on playing with myself, spreading my cum all over my length and using it as lubrication for another round.

I'm so revved up, it gets hard again pretty much straight away, but this one, the second time, is always the sweetest.

The second time is all about taking in the full joy of stroking and being denied release due to my male biology. So when Brody and our kiss plays out in my head, it goes on and on, getting bigger, wilder, sexier in my head.

He turns his back on me, but I press him toward me, my cock sliding between his cheeks. And before we know it, we're both naked in the middle of the Market, grinding, me possessing his neck with my tongue, biting his lobe, and feeling him weaken against me.

And then I drop him over his counter and insert myself nice and bare in his ass, and he's so tight that I come inside him within seconds while he screams my name for everyone to hear.

And as the fictional people of Burlington applaud our sensational performance, I spill again and my whole body goes numb, my muscles feeling like mash and my eyes heavy as fuck.

I wipe myself clean with a towel, then succumb to my exhaustion and get some rest. Although, not from Brody's phantom who lingers in my dreams one way or another.

I wake up the next morning, and while I'm showering, I go through yesterday's events with a clear head.

The way Brody looked at his ex, the way he froze as soon as he talked to him, how vulnerable and helpless he looked.

I had to help him. And shove it to the twat that dared cause a scene when he was the one to dump Brody in the first place.

It was probably a dick move to grope him. I never do stuff like that. Consent is important to me. There was probably a better way to help the poor guy, but that was the first thing that came to my head, and I acted on it without a second thought.

No wonder the guy was pissed at me. Even if he was the one to initiate the kiss that drove him over the edge.

That surely isn't going to cut me any favors with my game plan, so it's probably wise to apologize.

And show him my sweeter side.

Maybe if I explain my reasoning, he won't be so mad at me for what I did, and he'll get to see a more compassionate side of me.

Hopefully, that should also give me a chance to get to know him and find out what makes him tick.

After all, I have a bet to win. I can't do three months without sex. I haven't touched a guy in two whole days, and I'm already itching for connection. I can't imagine what it must be like to go without it for so long.

When I get out of the shower, I get dressed and sit at the dining table with my laptop and go through my emails.

Nothing new. Nothing important.

Which leaves me with one more thing to do before I head out.

I open the blank document and put my fingers over the keyboard, typing *Hard Rebound with the Sugarmaker*. I add a couple of returns and then pause.

I have a title. Now where's the rest?

I know I want to write about a friendly bet. And about a guy just like Brody. But how do I start?

He was hard and horny when he woke up, his dick way too abandoned since his fiancé left him at the steps of the local church.

I stop typing, and before I even read back my sentence, I hit the backspace button until it disappears.

This isn't right. It feels wrong. Intrusive.

I'm not sure why. It wouldn't be the first time I make up my own version of history for the guys I fuck. I may not spend much time learning what's brought them to my bed, but I use any tidbit of information I can garner and let my imagination go wild and free from there.

But for some reason writing Brody's past feels wrong. It feels perverted.

No. I need more to go on. I can't write this guy's story without knowing a little more about him.

I need to know what hides behind that grumpy face and what his smile really looks like. That should be enough to get my writing mojo back.

"Right," I say and shut my laptop.

It's time for some research.

I take out the wine I bought from him yesterday and crack it open.

The smell of alcohol turns my stomach so early in the day without any proper breakfast, but I still grab a wine glass from the cupboard and pour myself a few generous drops.

I've never heard of maple wine in my life, so I don't really know what to expect or how it's supposed to be drunk, so I do what I know from wine tasting.

I swirl the glass in my hand and put the rim under my nose to sniff.

The smell of oak and spice invades my senses, as does the earthy scent of the molasses.

I have a sip and swirl it in my mouth until it hits all the taste buds on my tongue. It's light, but sweet, a cross between maple syrup and dessert wine with a touch of whiskey.

I'm quite surprised. I was expecting... Well, I don't know what I was expecting, considering I've never tried maple wine before, but I like it.

I like a guy with layers, and his product certainly has them.

39

I put the glass down and grab the bottle again. One sip is enough at this time of day. I can get back to it later.

I read the label and all the small print, but I don't find much to go on other than the region, the ingredients, and the alcohol percentage.

No address, no website, no contact information.

Intriguing. Who in this day and age doesn't have any information on their product? Maybe it's not needed for the places he supplies to in small-town Vermont, but what about visitors, tourists, or people who end up with a bottle by chance?

I open my laptop again, ignoring the blank document in favor of the internet.

I type out the name of the wine, but all I get is a bunch of entries about maple syrup and a couple on maple wine.

Adding his name to the search, I try again but without better luck.

"Mr. Mercier, show some mercy. You're a hard man to find," I say to the search result page.

Well, when the internet fails—is that even a thing anymore —the grapevine will have to do.

So out I go, and other than a stop for a quick English breakfast at the local pub, I head straight for V&V and ask for Brody's address.

Harrison sends me to Tanner, Tanner goes through his invoices but can't find the one we're looking for, so he sends me to a restaurant called Bistro Charme. The guy barely recognizes the name, let alone gets me an address.

I end up hopping from shop to shop, trying to get any breadcrumbs to make a meal out of, and after a hell of a morning, I finally get somewhere.

I get Brody Mercier's address, which is outside of town. And I head right for him in my rental.

I've never worked so hard for a hookup. This guy better be ready to spread his legs for me today and let me rim him to show just how sorry I am for my behavior yesterday.

Because I'm hungry for some action, and I've got a book to write, after all.

BRODY

"Let's make today a great day, Mercier," I say to myself when I walk into my distillery.

My smoked whiskey barrel will be arriving tomorrow, and I'm ready to do some blending until I find the perfect mix to add to it. I'm so excited; my hands are twitching.

I start by taking a sample from each of my five existing casks and sit down at my lab table to do some taste testing.

I split each sample into five glasses and mix some together with others, while also keeping some pure samples from each cask. There's no rushing this process, and there's no such thing as being familiar with the flavors. Every day the maple wine sits in its cask changes its taste. Even when I think I know what I'm gonna get, it takes me by surprise. Which is why note-taking is my best friend.

By early afternoon, I have all my basic notes for each mix as well as a ton of other ideas floating about on the table.

"I'm hungry," I say to one sample as I take a big sniff of its aromas. "I wish I'd brought a snack. But if I walk away now, I'll lose my train of thought."

I wish that one of these days any of the things I talk to

would talk back to me. But they never do. They say that's the first sign you're going crazy. I say when that happens, it'll be the first time I don't feel alone in a long while.

"Oh, you're going to be gorgeous once you mature a bit more," I say to the next sample.

"Thank you. Although I do think I'm quite dashing now," someone says behind me in a breathy voice that makes me jump.

I drop the glass and hold on to the table before I punch my chest a couple times trying to kickstart my heart.

"I'm sorry. I knocked, but you didn't answer," the same voice says, but all I can focus on is the mess in front of me.

Not only did my glass topple over, spilling all the good juices, it also knocked a couple more glasses and got my notes all wet and smudgy.

Just as I was about to decide which was the best mix to put into my new barrel.

"Is this a bad time?" the voice asks when I let out a growl, and I finally turn around to see who has the audacity to interrupt me during important work.

Sure, no one else thinks it's important work, but I do.

I find myself looking at the silver-fox from the other day. The stranger who shoved his tongue in my mouth and made me forget my name for a moment.

"What have you done?" I growl at him.

He opens his eyes in surprise and approaches me, leaving the door of the distillery open. "Did you grow up in a tent? Shut the door."

I don't have the time to see if he obeys my orders, because I turn my attention to the table and try to salvage the notes on the ideal mix of maple wine.

I reach for a stack of papers and dab the wet patch, but that makes my hands sticky.

"Goddammit," I grind under my teeth.

"Here," says the guy and passes me a dry towel.

I snatch it out of his hands and wipe up the wine. When the table looks halfway decent again, I drop the towel to the floor and lift the wet piece of paper in my hands.

It's no use. It's all gone. All of today's work.

"Are you all right?" the guy asks.

"Do I look all right?" I ask, snapping my head at him. "I've been working all fucking day, and you just ruined it."

He looks at the table, and all the other samples that haven't been affected by my little spillage, and grimaces.

"I'm sorry. I didn't mean to—"

"What do you want?"

His steely gaze returns to me as his hands slide into his back pockets, brushing the grimace off his face.

"I came over to apologize for my behavior yesterday," he says. "I didn't mean to grope you or offend you."

Did he just say he came to apologize? To me?

"Well, yeah, you shouldn't have done it," I tell him.

He nods.

"I know. I feel awful about it," he starts, and then bites the edge of his lower lip. "It won't happen again."

"Why would it?"

He shrugs, and there's a trace of a smirk on his face. Smug bastard.

"I don't like you," I tell him before I can filter the thought through my head.

His smirk grows bigger. *Ass.*

"That's fine," he says. "I tend to grow on people."

He finishes off with a little twitch in one eyebrow, and I almost snort.

"Is that supposed to make me fall all over you?" I ask him.

"Do you *want to* fall all over me?"

"I'd rather choke to death."

"I don't know about dying, but I've been known to make people choke," he says.

"Oh Lord, do you think because you're British that your lines work better?"

I cross my hands and raise an eyebrow, waiting for this idiot in front of me to answer and get to the point of his visit here.

"I don't, no," he says. "But they tend to work better than they seem to with you."

He smudges his face, and I almost punch him.

"Are you trying to tell me that I'm the problem?"

"Of course no—"

"Because let me tell you, your lines are lame. As. Fuck. And I cannot believe they work on anyone. Now will you tell me why you so rudely interrupted my work? The real reason."

He watches me with half-slitted eyes, his chest rising and falling for a few seconds before he opens his mouth.

"That was it. I came here to apologize. No lies," he says.

I shake my head and turn my back to him, walking away to my office.

"I find it hard to believe a man like you wasted an hour of his life to come up here for an apology," I tell him and take a seat at my desk, putting a barrier between him and me.

He puts his hands on my desk and towers over it, and I'm feeling tiny all of a sudden. *Whose great idea was it to sit down*?

"An hour? Mate, you know how many hours I spent trying to find your address? Terrible marketing if you ask me. No website. No address anywhere. Hell, no restaurant in Burlington seems to even know your name," he says.

"I *will* punch you." The words escape my lips. "Did you come here to apologize or make me feel like shit?" I add before

45

he can comment. He may not look dangerous, but the last thing I need is to invite a fistfight.

"No," he says and deflates. He sits down on one of the chairs opposite me and drags it closer to the desk. "I'm sorry. I was trying to say I spent all morning trying to find you and apologize."

"And you want a gold star for the effort?" I ask.

Okay, I may be a bit hard on him, but...

He spent a whole morning trying to find me? Me? Brody-slash-Nobody-slash-Mercier?

I couldn't even keep a regular guy and this mountain of a hunk wasted his time on little ole me?

There's something odd going on here.

"No," he says. "Well...yes. That was my thought originally. But..."

"But..." I hum after him.

He takes a deep breath and licks his lips, placing his hands on top of the desk, reaching out for mine in the middle.

"But after a God-awful morning, I want to help you," he says.

"Help how?"

"With your business," he says.

"Excuse me?" I pull my hands back before he gets a chance to touch them. "Who do you think—"

"What I meant was..." he starts and raises his hands to halt my reaction. "I've got experience with branding and marketing and I can offer you my expertise."

Doesn't this sound terribly familiar. I wonder where I've heard that before. Oh, that's right, from the man who left me at the altar.

"I don't need help," I tell him.

"I beg to differ," he says.

"Well, I don't care what you think. I don't even know your name."

"Oh God, you're right. How rude of me. Logan Graves," he says and reaches his right hand across the desk. "Pleasure to meet you."

I take his hand with some hesitation, and he proceeds to kiss the back of it like they do in those old films. And even though I should feel insulted, I get tingles on the back of my neck and the top of my head. The trace of his lips on my knuckles stays there long after his corporeal lips have been removed.

Snap out of it, Brody. You're not falling for this guy's charms.

"Thanks for the rude interruption, *Logan*. I really don't know how I could have stretched my workload any further without you. You can leave now. I don't need a marketing consultant," I tell him.

"I really feel like I can help you," he says, and I get up from my chair.

He may be taller, but it's time I showed him who's boss around here.

"And I really feel like kicking your balls," I say. "We're done here."

So what if I still feel all tingly inside. From a fucking kiss on the hand for fuck's sake.

I'm as hopeless as my business.

LOGAN

Well, this visit went to plan.

All right, I didn't come up here with a plan, that's fair enough, but I didn't expect everything I said to aggravate the situation further.

It's a shame we can't have a do-over. Or pretend the last couple days didn't happen and start afresh.

The worst part is the guy really does look like he needs help, and I can offer it to him. For free.

Well, almost free, but that is definitely up to him, and my ability to get him into bed.

I didn't spend the best half of my twenties and thirties working in marketing for nothing. Thank God my writing took off when it did because if I had to sit in another room with posh, pretentious marketing gurus and wanker CEOs, I'd probably die of boredom.

I want to tell him all these things, but I don't think they'll do me any favors. He seems to have taken an instant dislike to me, and I've only gone and made it worse by telling him he needs help.

I'll have to find a different way to win this bet and quench my hunger for the handsome grump, but whatever way that is, it isn't happening today.

So with one last look at him, I get up, turn around, and start for the door.

"See you never," Brody says behind me, but I ignore it. He's just being extra to shove it in my face, and I can't say I blame him.

Before I can take more than a couple of steps, the door to this... Is it a lab? A distillery? A sugarhouse? I have no clue. Whatever it is, the door slides open and the same twat from yesterday walks in.

Brody's ex.

As soon as he sees me, he flinches and glares.

I don't know what the fuck he's doing here, but I think I just found my way into Brody's bed.

I cross my arms and stare back at the arse, putting on my best jealous-boyfriend face. Not that I have much experience with the look—or the feel—but I'm sure it's not hard to master.

"What the hell are you doing here?" I ask him.

Addressing him jolts him out of his frozen state and he furrows his brows.

"I could ask the same thing," he replies.

"Oh you could, could you?" I bite back at him.

Neither of us moves. Instead he crosses his arms, too, and we start a staring contest that I have no intention of losing.

Oh, honey, it's on!

"Theo? Wh-what are you doing here?"

I hear Brody approach from behind me, until he's standing between both of us, his gaze focused on his ex.

"I came to see if you're okay," Theo replies, still staring at me.

Brody turns to look at me before he turns back to Theo.

"I'm fine. Wh-why wouldn't I be?" Brody asks him.

Theo lifts his shoulders and puffs his chest, like a feather-less peacock.

"You…were acting strange yesterday—" he starts, but Brody clicks his fingers in front of his face and the twat is forced to look at Brody. "I wanted to make sure everything was…okay?"

He makes sure to direct the last word at me. If he wants to play this game, then I'm about to beat his arse.

"Brody is fine. Thank you for stopping by. Don't do it again," I tell him, taking a step to stand by Brody's side. "Aren't you, love?"

I want to touch him, get myself wrapped up with his body and put this wanker in his place, but I can't do it again. Not without his consent. I just hope he has enough verve in him to stick it to this man, and that he takes advantage of my presence here.

"Huh?" Brody says and glowers at me.

What on earth happens to him every time his ex is around? It's like all that spark and sass he's got disappears and is replaced with this shy, confused kid.

"Baby?" I tell him. "Do you want me to kick this arse out?"

"What?" he asks.

"Excuse me?" Theo says.

I know I promised myself not to touch him again without his permission, but I'll be damned if I let this man get the better of Brody. So I put my hand around his back, resting it on his shoulder and pulling him closer to my chest.

"You are *not* excused," I tell Theo. "And you can go now."

Brody jerks in my arm, but he doesn't push me off him.

"I'm not going anywhere until I speak to Brody," Theo says and looks at the young man leaning on me.

"Whatever you have to say, you can say in front of me," I

say to Theo, putting a mild suggestion of a threat under my snarled words.

Theo takes a step closer to us, and he almost looks like he wants to square up to me, but he's too uncertain.

I don't know what he's got to be uncertain about. I *can* and *will* definitely kick his arse.

"This is private. Between me and him," he tells me at a lower tone that I *think* is supposed to scare me.

But his grammatically incorrect sentence just confirms exactly what he is. A sheep in wolf's clothing.

Brody tenses against me and, for a moment, I think I've overstepped my boundaries again and misread the signs.

"Spill it, Theo. Wh-What is it? We have…um…some *business* to get back to," Brody says, and he slides his hand from my chest to my stomach, sending shivers down my spine and waking up the *other* Mr. Graves.

Theo's eyes focus on Brody's hand, and I take as much pleasure from seeing the fool shocked as I do from feeling Brody's touch.

"Erm…" Theo starts.

Brody moves his hand a bit lower on my stomach, where the waistband of my jeans starts. I'm not sure if he's doing it because Theo is so horrified, or if he wants to take his chance to feel more of me. Whatever the reason, I like it. And I want more.

"Erm, what?" Brody asks.

Theo huffs and finally takes his eyes off the hand to look at his ex.

"Since when is this…?" he asks, waving his hand between us. "How did you…? Where did you…?"

He keeps getting distracted by Brody's hand, which Brody brings around to my hip. He brings his other hand around my waist and grips my ribs.

"I'm sorry?" Brody asks. "Is that what you came up here for? To ask me when I started dating again?"

Theo glances at Brody and nods with some uncertainty.

"I just thought you'd be…" he starts but cuts off, looking back at me, and it's then I realize what his intentions had been.

He saw us together yesterday, got ridiculously jealous, and he wanted to come and get some for himself. For old time's sake.

Or he had such a low regard for the man strapped onto me that he didn't think Brody could get a man to notice him again. Especially a man like me.

One way or the other, he came here for release. I've slept with hundreds of men. I know what every expression, every twitch, and hesitation means. And this man is screaming sex.

Well, he's not going to get sex or release. Not if I have anything to do with it.

Brody raises his head at me and slips his mouth open gently. He also moves his hand from my hip, bringing it up, tracing the side of my face with his forefinger.

"Baby," he whispers. "I'm sorry about him. I swear we'll pick up right where we left off as soon as he's gone."

Oh the promise. If only it were real. But I know he's just saying it for his ex's benefit and not to tease me.

Or maybe he can thank me for making the ex jealous by bending over? Yeah…I'd like that. I'd like that very much, please and thank you.

"Which is when exactly?" I snap at Theo. If Brody is serious about the promise, this man needs to go ASAP.

"Oh, you can't be serious, the both of you," Theo huffs again and rolls his eyes.

Brody goes still against me again before turning his attention to Theo.

"Why not, Theo? Why can't I be serious? Because I've found someone that actually makes me happy?"

"You don't mean that," Theo says.

"Why do you care if I do or not? You gave up your right to control my life when you stood me up in front of our family and friends."

"That's not what—"

"Then what? You came to brag? Because you thought you had one up on me with your little sugarmaker? Tell me, is it a fetish to get it on with sugarmakers, or did you do it on purpose because he's better than me?"

"Nonsense, handsome. No one's better than you," I rumble in his ear, and I see his breath catch.

"No. That's...that's not what I meant. I...erm...I just came to ask you..." Theo glances from left to right, so gobsmacked by the way he's being spoken to by a man he thought was still mourning his absence, that it's almost sad to watch. The operative word being *almost*.

"I came to ask you if you're going to the Wine & Harvest Festival?" His eyes pinpoint on something and light up. "That's why I came here."

He turns to Brody, and I look to my right where there's a small counter full of flyers and knick-knacks.

One of those flyers is a yellow piece of paper with Wine & Harvest Festival written across its length.

"The Wine and... Why?" Brody asks.

Theo shrugs and tries to smile.

"It's just...my Skyler is attending with his *incredible* maple cream, and I was wondering if you were going too. It-it might be a good opportunity to sell some of that inventory."

He glances at the back of the room, and I turn to look too. There are crates upon crates stacked on top of one another, making for a dizzying amount of stock.

So, no one knows him in town, he doesn't have a website, *and* he has a shit-ton of wine to sell. This guy really needs my help. But I still don't like the way Theo talks to him. So condescending and superior all of a sudden, when he'd been a bumbling fool two seconds ago.

I may not know the history between these two, but like fuck am I going to let this wanker come out on top.

"Oh, we were just talking about it, weren't we, babe? We were going to submit our application, but..." I pinch my eyes and raise an eyebrow at Brody. "We got distracted."

Brody grimaces.

"We were? We did?" he says.

I tug at his shoulder and press him to my chest before I look at Theo.

"You don't need to be modest, love. Especially not with *him* of all people," I tell him.

Theo bites the inside of his cheek with a huff and crosses his arms again.

"Well..." he hisses. "Skyler is most likely to win the Innovative Product Award, so we certainly can't miss it. It'll be...*great* to see you there."

"Great is subjective, of course," I tell him. "But I guess we'll see you there. Right, Brody? When you win the award with your wine?"

I feel the heat of his gaze and the panic in his lack of breath.

I want to shake him. To jolt him awake. Poke into his head and get him over this arsehole that's so obviously still affecting him. But I can't do that. Not while said arsehole is still here.

He has a great opportunity to shove it to him and get him to shake in his boots, but I don't know if he's going to take it. I don't know if he's got it in him where Theo is concerned.

"Definitely. We'll see you in Dover," he tells Theo, and we

watch him fumble with himself before he leaves us all alone again.

"What the fuck is wrong with you?" Brody says as soon as we hear the roar of Theo's engine outside, and he pushes me off him.

Well, this should be fun.

8

BRODY

"Why would you do that?"

I honestly still can't believe what just happened. My brain is still trying to process everything.

"Do what?" he asks with a hint of a smirk.

Does this man ever *not* smile? Is there ever a time that he's not amused by other people's misfortunes?

"Everything," I say. "And stop smiling. Ass."

His chest rises and falls as he takes a breath, and he puts his hands in his back pockets again. I'm starting to think it's a tick.

"You know what I hate?" he asks, so calmly it almost sounds out of place amidst the frenzy in my head.

"Huh?"

"I hate wankers who can't appreciate what's right in front of them until it's too late," he says.

"Once again, huh?" I ask because I have no clue how this is relevant.

He flicks his thumb over his shoulder at the door and frowns.

"Your ex?"

A laugh erupts out of me before I've even fully comprehended what he's saying.

"Please! You think Theo is jealous?"

"You think he came here to ask you about a festival?"

He crosses his arms, and the sheer volume of his muscle makes a knot form in my throat. Not to mention the fact he reminds me of what he said earlier.

"Thanks for that, by the way. Now I'll have to figure out a way to get out of it while still saving face."

"Why would you want to get out of it?"

"Because I don't want to lose. Not while his stupid boyfriend goes up and takes the award for best motherfucker in Vermont," I tell him.

To think that Theo came to brag! If only I could find myself again around him, I'd wrap my hands around his throat and show him.

"Well, then…we're not losing," he says, and I can feel the growl building out of me before he hears it.

"First off, *dude*, there's no we."

"He thinks there is," he says with a flick of his eyebrow.

"Smug jerk," I say just as I think it. *Great job, Brody.*

I need to learn to control my impulses. But living on your own for three months with no soul to talk to is sort of liberating. Albeit a little demented.

"Which brings me to my next point." I shrug off my concern. "Why do you insist on groping me and going all lovey-dovey when Theo's around?"

"If you think that's groping…" he mumbles, but a glare at him makes him stop before he finishes his sentence. "Well, isn't it obvious?" he asks instead.

"That you're a dick? It's perfectly obvious," I tell him and turn around, going back to my desk.

At least there I have a barrier between us. Something to protect me from kicking his ass. Or kissing it.

"He's an arse who has no concern for your well-being and pretends leaving you at the altar was 'no biggie.' And I don't like it," he says.

When I turn around, he's followed me to the desk, but he's not standing on the other side, he's right next to me.

"That's personal. Don't act like you know me. And I *don't* need your help. I'm no damsel," I grumble.

He puts his hands up and nods.

"I know you're not. And I know you don't need my help, but I'm offering it anyway."

"Why?"

"I told you. I don't like wankers like him. Or how he makes you feel every time you see him."

"What do you know about how he makes me feel? I barely know your name, and you think you have me pegged?" I'm shouting now.

I don't like it. I hate when my voice goes so loud and the scratch on my throat, but this man is driving me insane.

And that Adam's apple on him, the way it bobs when he swallows, makes me want to bite it off. Just so it stops moving about so arrogantly.

"I don't. But I'd like to," he says.

Why is he saying that? Why would *he* want to get to know *me*?

"Why? Just to make my jerk of an ex jealous?" I shout at him.

"No," he says. "Because I like you. And I like helping the people I...well, like."

"That's a lot of likes, Mr. Graves," I say in a pretend British accent. "I'm not sure you mean it so."

He moves his hands to grab my shoulders, but thinks

better of it before he touches me. Instead he covers one hand with his other in front of him.

"I'm not going to lie to you. I'd love nothing more than to lay you down and show you a good time," he says, and my entire body shudders. Did he just say that? To my face? "But I'm not a pig either. I can tell that guy gets under your skin, and I know it's none of my business, but I can see your little enterprise here is not doing well."

I open my mouth to give him a piece of my mind about his opinion, but he uses a finger on my lips, and its delicate sensation gives me pause.

"I can help you with both things. I worked in marketing for fifteen years, and in case you didn't notice, I'm quite the hunk. So you have an opportunity to hit two birds with one *bloody hot* stone. So what do you say?"

Wowzers. This guy thinks way too much of himself. And why is my dick even reacting to what he's saying? He's just being a major cocky jerk. And yet all my head can think about is how sexy we'd be pinned against the wall with his dick inside me and my teeth biting down on his bottom lip.

His blue eyes burn into mine with their intensity, waiting on me as if I'm the love of his life, holding his existence in my hands, and it only makes the images in my head dirtier.

"No," I tell him.

He blinks and his head flicks an inch in confusion.

"What do you mean no?"

I frown and take a step back. This proximity to him isn't doing me any favors.

"I mean no. As in N-O, no. Thank you for your 'concern' and your 'offer,' but now I have two messes to figure my way out of. Thanks to you," I say with as much resolve as I can muster.

This would all be so much easier if he weren't so handsome. In such a cocky way, of course.

I really don't have a thing for cocky men. They really don't do it for me. Which is why I cannot understand the deal with my body reacting to this particular cock.

"Oh," he says, his hands moving to his pockets. His jacket pockets this time. Not his pants'.

"Oh indeed. Now if you don't mind? Lots of work to do," I tell him.

He hesitates, the uncertainty in his face looking so alien in comparison to the man I've seen so far, that it almost makes me change my mind just so he can offer me that *stupid* smirk of his.

But I don't, of course. I'm not in the business of making nice with others. I have myself to take care of.

And right now, not only do I have to make up for all my lost work from this morning, but I also have to find an excuse for not going to the festival without letting Theo know it's because of him.

All thanks to this man in front of me. Logan Graves. The British asshole who seems to bring trouble everywhere he goes.

"Give me a call if you change your mind," he says, and puts a card on the desk before he walks away.

"Are you sure you're okay?" Mom asks.

I stab my meatball and mash it with my fork instead of eating it.

"For the hundredth time, Mom, yes," I say.

"Don't raise your voice at your mother," Dad says.

"Sorry," I mumble to my plate.

"Don't scold your son." Mom slaps Dad's hand because if they ever agreed on anything it'd be a miracle on earth. "You're not hungry?"

"Huh?" I say and look up at her. "Oh. Yeah. I am. I just...I have a lot on my mind."

Like all the work I need to catch up with tomorrow, retasting all the samples and blends until I find the one I lost today.

Or what I'm going to say to Theo when I don't show up at the festival.

Or how the hell I can get Logan Graves out of my mind? Because those images from earlier? Yeah, they're still assaulting my head every so often.

"Of course you do. You need to take some time off," Mom says.

"Mom," I groan.

"Don't 'Mom' me, mister. It's not tapping season. You've got all those bottles gathering dust. You can take some time off. Nothing bad is gonna happen."

"Harper!" Dad scolds.

Mom looks from me to him and pouts.

"Oh, you two are gonna drive me up the wall one of these days," she says and throws her napkin on the table.

"Don't make a scene," Dad tells her.

"I'm *not* making a scene. I'm his mother. I'm allowed to be concerned. Our son needs to rejoin civilization. He was jilted. I get it. But he can't let that stop him from living the rest of his life. He's only twenty-eight for crying aloud. Look at Theo. He's a douchebag through and through, and he acts like he's the bigger man, parading his new beau around."

"Mom!" I grumble.

"You can't let him be the bigger man, Brody. You need to

get yourself back out there. Go out. Meet people. Fall in love. We're not going to let Theo *fucking* Coggan win, are we?"

"What's with all the 'we' lately?" I ask.

First Logan is acting as if my business is also his business, and now Mom is talking as if Theo walked out on her as well as me.

"What do you mean? That boy let us all down. He embarrassed us all."

"And yet you're still besties with his mom," I say.

She kisses her teeth and her face sours.

"She *is* my best friend. It's not my fault or hers she raised an asshole. It's all that scum-of-the-earth dad of his to blame."

"Did you invite me for dinner to talk about Theo?" I huff.

Mom shakes her head and lifts her wine glass.

"I invited you for dinner so we can have dinner. *As a family*. You don't have to go through this alone, you know—"

"Harper!"

"Oh, I've had enough of you two. Now eat up so we can have pumpkin pie, Goddammit," she says and gulps her wine until it's empty.

Mom isn't kidding around today.

I let dinner pass quietly and so does Mom. Dad doesn't count because he barely ever talks and barely ever replies with anything but yes, no, or "Harper!"

When we're all sitting at the living room with a slice of pumpkin-and-maple pie, I decide to pick up the conversation again.

"Theo came by today," I tell them.

Mom covers her mouth with a napkin as she rushes to respond.

"And?" Dad asks.

"He had the audacity to come back? What the hell did he want?"

For a second, Logan's words cross my mind. His suggestion that Theo came around because he got jealous.

I dismiss the notion again.

"He wanted to ask me if I'm going to the festival in Dover. His precious Skyler is going."

"The fucking dickwad," Mom exclaims. "Did you tell him to go crawl back up his mother's vagina and never talk to you again?"

I try to laugh at Mom's joke, if it can even be called that considering she's referring to her best friend, and shake my head.

"No. He thinks I'm going. And now I need to find my way out," I tell her.

Mom puts her plate on the table and wipes her mouth before she sits next to me.

"Why would you find a way out? You're going," she says.

"I'm not. I'll just end up embarrassing myself."

"Brody Finnley Mercier, you are *not* letting that man win."

"He's already won, Mom."

"Nonsense. Just because he's got a boyfriend and a successful career doesn't mean he's winning."

"Oh yeah? And what do I have? No boyfriend and a lot of wine that will never sell. There's no contest."

"Bullshit," Dad says, and at first it doesn't register it's him. He rarely ever engages in our conversations—other than to tell Mom off, of course.

"What?" I ask him.

"You're acting like you've already given up on Grandad's farm. What would he say if he heard you? Huh?"

I take a deep breath and set my own plate down. It's highly unlikely I'm eating the rest of the pie now.

"He'd say to get my head out of my ass and go out there," I mumble.

"Damn right," he replies.

"It's not that easy, Dad. No one wants my wine."

"Then find someone who does," he says, and what is wrong with me that the first person my thoughts go to is a certain cocky British guy?

He said he wants to get to know me. He said that he likes me. Hell, he even admitted he wants to fuck me.

But he did also offer his help. Did he mean it?

He wouldn't be the first guy to come into my life and promise to help before abandoning me out of the blue.

"You said Theo's got a successful career?"

I don't know why my mind chooses this moment to click with what Mom said earlier, but it does, and I have to ask the question. Even if I don't like the answer.

"Well, yeah. He got a job at Harvey's."

"The real estate agent?"

Mom nods and resumes her pie-eating, obviously relieved enough at her husband's outburst of support that she feels her job here is done.

"But he's allergic to normal work," I say.

Hell, now I'm fuming.

Two years I begged that ass to find a job and stop gigging around trying to sell people lies and subscriptions, and he kept putting my concerns down, reassuring me he was close to hitting a goldmine.

And now that he left me, he decides to sort his life out?

Well, fuck that. And fuck him. Well…not actually fuck him. I'd rather fuck the other guy that has intruded into my life. Not that it's going to happen. I'm in no mood to fuck around, no pun intended.

"I have to go," I say and shoot up from the couch.

"What? What happened?" Mom asks.

"My ass is on fire," I tell her, and she laughs.

"There's a cream for that," she says.

I reassure her I'm fine, but that I need to go before I lose steam and change my mind again, and she packs up the rest of the pumpkin-and-maple pie to take with me. A gesture Dad is not happy with. He loves his freaking pie.

It takes me ten minutes to get home, and when I do, I run straight for the distillery and unlock the door.

I grab the card Graves left behind and call the number on my phone, roaming charges be damned.

As I wait for an answer and read his name on his plain white card with the golden lettering, the images from earlier pop up.

Those steely eyes staring right down at mine as his cock rips through me, weakening my entire existence.

"Hello," says a raspy voice on the other end, and if I wasn't horny before, I certainly am now.

"Hey," I mumble and clear my throat.

Get it together, Mercier.

"Logan Graves?" I ask, as if his voice could be mistaken for anyone else's.

"Brody Mercier!" he exclaims, and I drop my hand to my cock and give it a squeeze.

"Yup," I say.

"To what do I owe the pleasure?" he asks, and I almost moan as I imagine him on his knees, my cock on his lips as he asks me the same thing.

Damn.

I don't even have control of my hand as it reaches under my pants and grabs my bare cock.

"I...um...I thought about your of-offer," I say.

"You have? That's fabulous. I really meant what I said earlier. I can really help you."

"Uh-huh," I say, rubbing my length slowly.

"So, we still have a few weeks before the festival, right?"

"W-we do," I say.

"I've been looking into it. We'll need to call and ask about getting in because it might be late, but I can work my magic and get us in," he says, and I drop back in my chair, relaxing my body and letting his voice soothe the tornado in my head, but it only intensifies the tightness in my hand.

So of course I let him go on, but I release my cock from the constraints of my pants until it's exposed and free to rub.

"God, what am I doing?" I unintentionally say aloud and immediately let go of my cock to shut my mouth.

"No. Don't change your mind now," he says. He probably thinks I'm regretting calling him. If only he knew what I was really doing. "Listen, I don't do this often. But there's something about you. You've got a great product. You just need help with everything else. I promise you. I've done this long enough. I know…"

He continues to talk, trying to convince me of something I've already decided but was too afraid to admit to myself.

That I need his help just as much as I need him and both things could end up in a big disaster.

But fuck me if I can control myself and deny him. I can't even stop my hand from rubbing my cock, bringing me all the closer to release.

"Are you free tomorrow? I can swing by and we can get straight to work," he says, just as I shoot my load all over my shirt and finally allow myself to take a breath.

"Wh-what are you…up to?" he asks when I let out an unexpected gasp.

I sit up in my chair immediately and wipe my hand off on the side of my shirt.

"N-nothing," I say.

"Are you sure?"

Hell, did he install cameras in here or is my breathlessness so obvious?

"I'm sure," I say. "I just…I just came back from a jog."

A laugh comes from his side and rubs my ear with its arrogance. I can't believe I just came thinking of this jerk.

"If you say so," he says. "So…tomorrow?"

"Huh?" I ask.

"Tomorrow? Should I come over?" he says, and I let out a sigh of relief.

"Oh yeah. You can. I'm…I'm free," I say.

"Tomorrow it is then, handsome," he says and hangs up before I can tell him what time to get here.

And I have way too much pride to call again. Or send a message.

I guess I'll just have to wake up early and be ready for him.

Is something wrong with my brain? Because the moment I think about being ready for him, all I can picture is me in my bed, ass hanging over, waiting for his cock to enter me.

"I'm doomed." I slap my face.

9

LOGAN

The steam of my coffee rises from the cup and my fingers rest on the computer keys while I watch it climb the air until it disappears.

Monday morning traffic has started to creep out on Church Street and, for a few moments, I feel like I'm back in London looking out at the nearest High Street. Burlington wouldn't be entirely out of place planted somewhere in England. The red bricks, the low-rises, the cold weather.

My fingers start flying over the keys before I can overthink. Before I can put a cap on my words and the content.

I try to get into the head of a fictional social butterfly living on the busiest side of town and waking up one day to realize how alone they are, looking out of their window and seeing everyone go about their business when he has none. All he ever has for company, when it matters, is his music. His passion for notes, rhythm, and lyric. And no friend, relative, or lover can ever see the real person underneath, the one desperate to be needed, to be wanted, to be touched.

To be loved.

There's a certain space I go to when I'm writing, this space between reality and fiction, that I lose my senses and acquire new ones. When my thoughts aren't my thoughts at all, but someone else's. And my desires aren't mine, but a familiar stranger's.

Time moves differently there. It barely exists. My fingers have full control. Not me or my mind, but my hands. They are the conductors that create whatever magic they need to expel.

For the first time in months, I get lost in it. It snatches me away from Burlington, Vermont and drops me right in the middle of this stranger's soul, telling me what he feels, how he acts, showing me his deepest secrets that even he doesn't know he has.

The phone by my side goes off. It startles me. The ringtone pulls me out of the zone and back into the real world with a violent abandon.

"Hello?" I answer it, annoyed with whoever it is that's interrupting me.

"Hey, love. Is this a bad time?" Chloe asks on the other end of the line.

I look at my manuscript and the thousands of words I've managed to type.

"No. It's okay. What's up?" I ask her and get off the chair.

The more I look at my words, the more frustrated and worried I get that I won't be able to go back to that place I need to pick up the story.

"Oh, good. I've been waiting forever to call you, but I didn't want to wake you up," Chloe says, unaware of what she's done. "How's Vermont? Gorgeous guys?"

Brody's face comes up as soon as she mentions the word gorgeous and with that his call from last night comes to mind.

It had come out of nowhere, and so did the fact he was touching himself while talking to me. I'm no stranger to phone sex. I can read the signs. Or listen to them anyway.

Of course, sleeping after his call proved impossible until I had a go of the same inappropriate touching on myself, and even then I'm sure it didn't hold a candle to having the real thing with Brody.

"Brody!" I let out when I remember the nature of his call last night.

"Excuse me?" Chloe says as I scramble back to my laptop and check the time.

It's already way past ten. I wanted to get up there bright and early and show him I meant business when I talked about helping him.

"Nothing," I tell Chloe. "I just have somewhere to be and got…distracted."

"Ooh. Tell me more, tell me more," she says.

"Did you miss the part where I said I'm late?"

"Of course. Sorry. I'll get to the point then. Janet has been chasing me for an update," she says.

"She's being very pushy lately," I tell Chloe.

"Well, honey, you *have* missed your deadline twice now. She just wants to make sure the book is coming," she hums, and it's as if I'm sitting right across from my agent.

Chewing the end of her pen, prickled eyebrows, bright-pink lips leaving a mark on everything.

"It's coming, all right?" I say. "Fucking hell, you'd think I was a newbie or something."

"A newbie would have been dropped the minute they missed their first deadline, hon."

"That's right. How could I forget?" I say, as if I don't know my relationship with my publisher has been on the rocks lately.

"So? What should I tell her? What's your word count so far?"

I look at my screen and the number in the bottom of the

screen looking back at me is three thousand. The most I've written in four months. But it's hardly a Logan Graves book. It's barely even a Logan Graves chapter. There's no heat, no steam, no encounter as of yet. Just a character and his fucked-up thoughts.

"Nothing, yet," I tell her.

"Nothing?" she gasps. "What do you mean nothing?"

"Nothing, as in zero words," I respond, and just as I can sense her about to speak, I add, "But I've got an idea finally. So I'm working on it."

"Will you have enough time? I don't think I can ask Janet for another extension," she says. "I'm terrified she'll shoot the messenger."

"I can do it. Promise." A pang of guilt punches my stomach at the little white lie.

I still don't know if I can. But I'll damn well try. It wouldn't be the first time I had to whip up a book in six weeks.

"Okay, love. I'll tell her you're halfway through, though, to appease her. So you better finish it, or I'll kill you before she has a chance to shoot me," she says, and I hang up with a laugh.

I give the last few words on my laptop a read-through before I close the laptop and grab my coat.

I've got a trip to make and an adorably grumpy sugar-maker to help.

"I was starting to think you bailed on me," Brody says when I pull up in his drive, next to his pickup truck.

"Naw, and you've been standing out here since dawn?" I coo, resting an arm on the window for a moment before I get out.

"Pfft, please. Who do you think you are? The Queen of England?" he says, turning around and walking toward the distillery. "Come on. You got me into this mess. You need to get me out of it."

I follow behind him, and we escape the chilly Vermonter autumn in the warm and quiet warehouse.

"So…" Brody says, and he plonks himself behind his desk.

I sit opposite him and cross my legs with a smile.

"So?"

His brows furrow deeper and he leans forward.

"So what are your plans for my wine? You said you can help with marketing. Where do we start? Books, magazine ads, TV? Just an FYI, billboards are not a thing in Vermont so that's out of the quest—"

"How about we start from the beginning?" I ask, and he stops with his mouth open, waiting for me to go on.

"We need to get into the festival first, so how about we do that before it's too late?"

"Right." he says. "The festival. Of course."

He grabs a flyer from his desk drawer and passes it over to me.

"You can use the landline if you want," he says. "Do you want some coffee?"

He stands up and stares down into my eyes while waiting for a response. I could have taken a picture of his beautiful brown eyes. The way they hang onto me waiting for a response with mild irritation. That's all it takes to get me riled up. Those eyes. That scowl. That futile resistance to me.

"Coffee would be fantastic, thank you," I say, and he nods.

"Cream?"

"When you say cream do you mean normal cow milk or fatty cream?" I ask him, remembering the weird American habit of calling anything dairy that goes in coffee "cream," which was how I once ended up with butter in my coffee.

"I have both," he says. "And half-and-half. Or maybe you'd like an Irish coffee with some maple wine in it."

He says it with an extra sparkle that I haven't seen on him before.

"Just the milk, thanks," I reply, and he wanders off back into the main house, disappointment written across his face.

I get back to the task at hand, and it turns out registering for the event is easier than I had anticipated, so by the time Brody comes in with the coffees, I've already received the application form in my email.

"Here you go," he says and passes me a cup.

With the liquid boost, we print and fill in the form and it's sent off before we get down to real business.

"What's next?" he asks, settling back in his office chair.

I scan the room and my gaze falls on the countless crates stored in the back.

"How many do you have?"

He shrugs.

"More or less? Ten thousand bottles," he says.

My jaw drops before I can even control it.

"Please tell me they're not already labeled," I say with mild concern in my voice.

"Of course they are," he says. "Ready to sell."

Yup, it's just as I feared. My job just got a hundred times harder.

"You are definitely not going to like the next matter at hand," I tell him.

Brody turns his full attention to me, eyes slitted and hands crossed on his desk.

"Which would be?"

"Your name," I tell him.

"Brody Mercier," he replies.

I shake my head with a mild chuckle to lighten the mood, but I don't think it works.

"I meant the name of your product. Of your company."

"What's wrong with it?" he grumbles with a cup in front of his mouth, as he's about to take a sip.

I purse my lips and straighten up in my chair.

"How about we start with your story," I tell him.

Part of me is terrified of offending him again. When people's businesses are failing, their insecurities tend to strengthen and mold into this awful overprotectiveness. And considering we've already started off on mostly the wrong foot, I don't want him to shut me off again. Not after how much it has taken me to even get close to him.

I haven't worked so hard for a shag in the history of ever.

But that's the other part of me. It enjoys the challenge of cracking such a tough nut. Finding out what makes him tick and what makes him unravel.

He's probably going to be my toughest challenge to date, and I can't wait to see how this turns out. And what kind of book I get out of it.

"Story?" he asks, interrupting my absent-mindedness.

"Yes. Your story. Who are you? What motivated you to start this business? What keeps you moving forward?"

Brody readjusts on his chair and his gaze drops to his hands.

"What does that have to do with anything?" he asks.

"It's got *everything* to do with your products. People don't buy out of necessity. They buy out of connection. If they can't connect to your story, they won't care what you sell. Especially for maple wine," I say, and he interrupts me with a cry.

"What's wrong with my wine?"

"There's nothing wrong with your wine. In fact, for what

it's worth, it's actually surprisingly good. But no one knows that. Because all they see when they look at your bottles is a weird name and no personality."

"Are you gonna keep insulting me, or are we actually going to do some work?" he grumbles.

"I'm sorry," I say and offer him my trademark smile, but it only seems to irritate him further. "I don't mean any offense. It's just… Well, if people can't get past the name, they won't even pick up a bottle. And then they will never get to experience the brilliance of your drink."

"My name is fine," he says. "It was my grandad's name. And if it worked for him, it'll work for me."

I hit a goldmine without even meaning to.

"Talk to me about your grandad," I tell him.

If I was in a client meeting, I'd have a notebook and pen in front of me, ready to take all the notes.

But something tells me if I do that with him, he'll just stop talking and shut me out. So I'll have to rely on my memory.

"He was the best human in the world," he says with a deep scowl and sits back on his chair. "I spent most of my life on this farm while my parents worked their asses off to make ends meet. He taught me everything I know."

"Oh yeah? Like what?" I smile at him.

He gazes at something to his left and his face softens as he sinks further into his seat.

"He showed me how to tap a maple tree when I was only five," he starts. "How to measure and calculate. Then we'd bring the sap back here and put it through the reverse osmosis system, and he'd walk me through the process of making syrup."

There's a hint of a smile on him, and I want to coax more of it out. He already looks hot as fuck when he glowers, but I can see that his smile will make him even hotter.

"Syrup?" I ask. "What about the wine?"

"Oh, that was his hobby. Something he liked to do on the side. He always had some spare maple syrup, so he started fermenting it and experimenting with it. The rest of the syrup he sold to local brewers and producers who wanted to create other stuff," he says.

An inkling of a new name is already itching at the back of my head, but it's too early to tell.

"Do you still sell the syrup? How come you're not bottling and selling pure maple syrup?"

He shrugs.

"Because everyone is already doing that. And I don't have a big enough sugar farm to make much of a dent in that market. I thought the wine was something different. That it'd stand out. I thought I could make it into something new and exciting. A lot of people seem to be making their own maple wine with water and yeast at home these days. Something to enjoy with friends and family. I wanted to make it into a craft. I wanted to make Grandad proud. To make his secret passion a blooming business."

"What was his name?" I ask him.

I'm so close to that new name, I can almost taste it.

"Oh, you're gonna laugh. His name was Broderick. Or Brody, for short, which is what my parents decided to name me," he says.

"That's amazing," I tell him and sit up on my chair, excited to share my revelation with him.

"Really? It's not that uncommon to be named after an older family member," he says as some of the frown returns to his face.

But only some.

"That's not what I meant," I say. "Tell me, what comes to mind when you hear Mercier Wine?"

Brody crosses his hands and tightens his lips from side to side, staring at me.

"Innovation. Quality… Care," he says.

I nod, my lips curving into a smile.

"Now what does Brody's Secret Maple Wine make you think?"

He widens his eyes and his mouth drops.

"Family secret," he says. "Mysterious. Intriguing. What the fuck?" he shouts.

"What?" I ask, concerned at his change of tone.

"How the fuck did you convince me in two seconds that I need to rename my wine?"

I laugh and sit back on my chair.

God, he had me worried there for a second.

His shocked expression turns back into a scowl, but his lips? They form a smile I desperately want to kiss.

"Damn it, you're good," he says.

Oh, dear Brody. You have no idea how good.

BRODY

"What is it, Mom?" I ask when she doesn't get to the point.

I have a very giddy Logan in front of me, who almost looks sexy. If he wasn't so completely creepy with his stupid smirky face and all.

And I can't wait to see what's got him so excited. Not that it takes much to get him excited, I've come to realize. Talking, walking, or hell, even sitting in silence makes him happy. I'd say it's infectious if it wasn't so completely disgusting. Feelings and shit.

"Is that how you talk to your mother now?"

"That's how I always talk to you, Mom. When you don't. Get. To the point!" I huff, and Logan pouts with a furrowed brow.

"Well, Mrs. Norwich's daughter got engaged," she says.

"And I care about Mrs. Norwich's daughter, whom I haven't seen in eight years, why exactly?"

I take a breath when I finish and turn my back on Logan. There's something about the way he looks at me every time I talk that I don't like. I don't know if it's amusement, frustration, or curiosity. It annoys me any which way.

"Oh, stop it. You and Amy practically grew up together. And she was at your wedding... Anyway, they're throwing a little barbeque party while the weather's still good, and they have invited all of us," she says.

"I'm busy, Mom. I won't be able to make it," I tell her.

And it's not even a lie. Changing the name of my wines is only the beginning. There's a God-awful thousand of bottles that need relabeling. Once we get the logo sent through. And that's only the start of Logan's plan. I don't even know what he's got in store for me next.

"You *have* to go. Theo will be there," she says.

"Then I'm definitely not going," I tell her.

"Oh, sweetie, come on. Remember what we talked about the other day? How you can't let him win? If you completely withdraw from all social life because of him, then he definitely wins."

"Okay. Okay. I'll think about it," I tell her.

"You're coming."

"Mom! I'm not going to a party my ex is attending just because you say so. Now I said I'll think about it. I need to go. We'll talk later."

I hate it when she's forcing decisions on me. I know it's that motherly love she can't control that wants the best for me, but sometimes I wish she'd let me decide myself what's best for me. I *am* an adult after all.

"Okay. Are you coming for dinner tonight?" she asks.

I turn back to Logan and find him patiently waiting for me to hang up.

"Maybe," I tell her. "I really *am* busy."

"Well, I've made your favorite. So you better get here before your father eats it all," she says, and I promise to let her know later. On both dinner and party.

"Hey," I say to Logan, finally.

"Hey back," he says.

He sits in the office and retrieves a laptop from its case.

"What was that all about?" he asks.

I shake my head and sit across from him.

"Nothing. She wants me to go to a party Theo is going to. You'd think it was her he left at the altar instead of me," I tell him, then remember I don't owe him an explanation, so I seal my lips shut, glaring at him.

"Well, she is your mother, and she loves you very much, so he may as well have stabbed her in the heart too," he says.

I don't answer him. I just stare at his "perfect" blue eyes that have so much verve they scare me.

"Anyway. That party sounds perfect," he says.

All I do is arch an eyebrow and cross my arms, leaning on the desk.

"We want to stick it to him, right?" he starts but pauses. "You. Sorry. *You* want to stick it to him? So why not go?"

Does he even need to ask? What's wrong with him?

"Because what do I have to stick it to him? Oh yeah, I've renamed my wine. Look at me winning at life," I grimace and fall back in my chair.

"You've got me," he says, and there's no smile, no spark in his eyes. Just the intensity of his statement as it is.

"I...I got you?" I stammer. "H-how?"

"Doesn't Theo think we're together?"

My head barely moves an inch, but somehow he sees my nod and goes on.

"Well, then we go to this party, and we show him how well you're winning at life, as you say," he tells me and leans forward, the smirk back on his face.

"That lasted long enough." The thought escapes me, confusing Logan. I try to ignore it. Maybe if I don't make a big deal out of my random outbursts, he won't notice *or* remember them. "You don't have to do that. I'm sure you've got plenty of shit to do. And you're already wasting your time here with me, teaching fish how to swim."

"Was there…" He grins. "Anything else you'd like me to teach you?"

His tongue almost pops at the last word, and my whole body tenses.

Logan Graves is *not* attractive. Or if he is, I don't find him so. His muscles are too big and fake, his eyes are too blue, his hair is too perfectly streaked black and white as if it's intentionally dyed that way, and his arrogance is off the charts. While the look of him may be attractive, he's the least attractive guy I've ever seen.

So why the hell can't I stop drooling every time I look at him.

"Don't be crude," I shoot him down with all the spite I can muster.

It's the only alternative to letting him know how oddly aroused I am.

"Sorry, but you literally gave that to me willy-nilly," he says, and as much I try to keep the façade, I crack up.

"Willy-nilly?" I laugh.

"You know, willy is also a euphemism for—" he starts.

I raise my hand in front of him and cut him off.

"I know what it means," I say. "Idiot."

I try to erase any signs of entertainment on my face and replace it with my business look.

"Right. I'll get serious again," he says. "The point I was trying to make is you have the chance to parade me in front of everyone and make that jerk wish he could delete himself and his mistake from existence. So why not take it?"

He has a point. Although, I also think I have a point about not going to the party, but I can't remember it now.

That asshole hurt me. And I really enjoyed seeing the regret on his face when he saw me in Logan's arms over the last few days.

"Fuck it. Why not."

"Perfect," Logan says and slaps the wooden surface with cheer. "How about dinner tonight?"

"Excuse me? Is that the only reason you suggested it? To get me to go to dinner with you?"

"No," he says, but he's smirking again. Does he even realize he does it, or is it plastered permanently on his face out of overuse? "But if we're going to pretend to be a couple, we need to know more about each other, don't we? I thought dinner might be a great chance to do it. While also showing others that you've got someone. If I've learned anything in my short time here, it's that everybody talks."

"Forget it," I tell him.

"I guarantee I'm a true gentleman," he says with a little too much conviction for my liking.

"Really? I haven't seen proof of that."

He laughs.

"Well, no one said I'm a gentleman one hundred percent of my time. I'll leave you to decide what other things I am," he says.

I'm losing my patience with him. And with my body for betraying me and reacting so cruelly toward me. Why am I even hard now? Is there a reason? Like an actual reason?

"Are we gonna get to work or what?" I ask him in an effort to distract my mind from picturing him in every possible position in my bed.

His eyes flicker and he opens his laptop.

"Yes, sorry. You distracted me," he says.

He tends to apologize a lot, I've noticed, but I've yet to see if he means it. "I got an email back from my friend…"

He turns the laptop around and shows me the screen which is filled in black. Brody's Secret Maple Wine is written across the middle in front of a golden box. An equally gold maple leaf is on top of the words and the sides are filled with the ingredients, ABV, provenance, and social media links. Social media I don't really have.

"That's beautiful," I tell him, looking at the bottle on my desk with the old label in its parchment white and brown colors. "It doesn't compare. But how? We only came up with the idea yesterday."

"He...he's an old friend. He'll do *anything* I ask him," he says, and I detect a hint of pride in his words.

"This is amazing," I tell him, unable to stop staring at the new label and logo. "Thank you. So much."

"Oh, we haven't started yet," he says and pulls the laptop away.

"Wh-what's next?"

He looks at the bottle on my desk and smirks.

"You still haven't given me an official tasting," he says. "You seemed to be doing one on Sunday when I interrupted you. I take it you're experimenting with the best batch?"

"No. The normal batch is the standard. That's the one I bottle and sell. But I have some other casks I use to experiment with. I'm trying to produce something smokier and stronger. Kinda like a whiskey or a liquor. Something that can be enjoyed on the rocks."

Logan whistles and arches his eyebrows in a show of surprise and admiration that doesn't help my boner situation in the slightest.

"That definitely will have market appeal too. I am certainly happy to be your guinea pig," he says.

"How about muscle?" I ask him instead.

"Excuse me?"

"I need help moving my new barrel into the barrel room. I could use your muscles. You know. Unless they're just for show," I goad him.

"Lead the way, love." He grins.

And I do. Trying to hide the ever-growing erection in my pants.

Since when do I like big, burly jerks that think way too much of themselves?

"I don't like him," I tell myself.

Shit. Did I say that aloud?

"Did you say something?" Logan asks, stepping up next to me.

"No," I shake my head. "Just…erm…just…"

Think, Brody. Think.

"How much I don't like my ex."

"Oh, aha," Logan says. "Is there anyone you *do* like?"

"Pfft. Of course not. Men and me? Done." I dust my hands to emphasize my point.

"Are you going to date women?" He smirks.

"God no," I say. "I…um…I'm not dating anyone. Not that it's any of your business."

He surrenders and puts his hands in his back pockets.

"Hey, you started talking about it."

"Well…" I say. "Shut up. And help me."

I point him to the cask that needs to be set up.

"Oh, baby, that's what I'm doing," he says and winks at me.

Winks!

The fucking nerve of him.

He leans over the cask and the jeans tighten on his butt, drawing my gaze to those two perfect globes.

"Fuck," I groan. I'm never getting rid of this boner, am I?

"Did you say something?" Logan cocks his head and there's that stupid smirk on his face.

God I want to punch it so bad.

"Nothing. I said, 'fuck you.'"

"Or me fuck you. I'm easy."

"No more talking," I inform him, feeling the heat on my cheeks.

"I can do that too. I've always had a thing for quiet sex. Especially if it's paired with some cheeky public location." He stands up and leans against the cask he's supposed to be moving.

"Um…" I say, but I can barely think straight with the direction this conversation has gone. "Let's um…let's get one thing straight, Mr. Graves. Just because you're helping me with my wine and pretending to be my boyfriend *does not* mean you get to sleep with me. Or joke about it—"

"I wasn't jok—" he interrupts.

"I'm still talking. You may have shoved your way into my life, but I am not yours for the taking. Clear?"

"Crystal," Logan grins.

"Now move the fucking cask."

LOGAN

Another early morning passes in front of my laptop, and I can finally feel the fog in my head, the one that's been torturing me for months, shifting.

The words are flowing and the book is writing itself.

Only it's not the book I'm supposed to be writing.

My brand is sexy, steamy, erotic.

And that is not what I currently have. I have two characters who are denying their attraction and being stubborn as all hell just trying to get them into a hand job, let alone into bed.

It needs fixing. That's for sure.

And my bet isn't progressing any better.

That's what it is. That's why the characters are refusing to cooperate. I need the inspiration Brody offers. All of it. And since he turned down my offer for dinner, I'll have to up my game.

So after a good session, where I manage to knock out another few pages, I go out shopping just as Church Street springs to life, and when I pull up at Brody's, I'm determined this will be the day I win my bet.

"Morning," he says when I walk in.

I can see a hint of a smile. It's almost there, and I can't wait to edge it fully out of him. I bet it suits him much better than the scowl he's got permanently glued on his face. Even if it's also quite the look on him.

"Good morning, babe," I say, and any hint of a smile is gone, replaced by an inquisitive frown. "Honey? Sweetheart?"

His frown turns into a grimace and he takes a step away from me toward the barrel room.

"What are you doing?" he grumbles.

"I'm just testing things out. I *do* need to find your pet name, don't I?" I smile at him.

"You do, do you? Why?"

He opens the door to the barrel room, and I follow him inside as he stands in front of the first of his six barrels.

"Did you forget the part where we're attending a party as a couple and we need to look—and sound—convincing?"

He barely reacts to my words. Instead he kicks the first wedge under the barrel. Then he kicks the other one and puts both hands on top of the wooden container and rolls it to the opposite wall, then proceeds to kick the wedges back into place. He may be smaller than me, and his muscles half the size of mine, yet he barely flinches at the laborious task.

It's hot, and I can't help but feel a little turned on watching him get to work.

"Just call me Brody," he says when he's done. "What's with the bag?"

He looks down at the reusable bag I came in with, and I set it down to help him with the next barrel. As hot as it is watching him, I don't think observing will do me any favors.

"I brought some stuff so I can cook lunch for you," I tell him.

We each kick a wedge from under the barrel and move it to

the wall opposite, the splashing of the liquid inside offering some sort of response to the silence in the room.

"You don't have to cook lunch for me," he says, looking down at the floor.

"I want to," I say. "I want to get to know you."

He glances at me before he turns his back and walks to the next barrel.

"Why? We're not really dating."

Maybe not, but that doesn't mean I don't want to know the real Brody. The one underneath the gruff appearance and the twink-lumberjack look. It would make my character based on him more realistic.

And besides the book, I want to know him for me. People have always fascinated me. What motivates them. What scares them. It's one of the reasons writing has become my calling.

"Still. We can discuss things I'd know about you if we were dating. We wouldn't want to make up a surfing trip if you can't swim for example," I say instead.

"Whatever," he mumbles. "We've got work to do for now."

And so we get to work.

We move the rest of the barrels, including the oak one that I helped him set up yesterday, which he has filled with water until he finds the best blend for it. Once we're done, we move to the office and talk labelling.

He thinks placing a small order for labels is the best course of action until he can see if the new branding will work at the festival. It takes a bit of marketing speak and a lot of nudging, but I'm finally able to convince him to order the thousands of labels he'll need to rebrand all the bottles. Once we set up an order with Auden from the letterpress studio in Burlington, I turn around and put a time-out on our work for the day.

"It's lunch time," I tell him.

He rolls his eyes and lets out a big sigh, but he gets up.

"Fine," he says and walks toward the door connecting the distillery to the house I haven't been in yet. "But only because I'm starving."

He points a finger at me, and I so want to...

"That's the whole point of lunch, you know. To appease the hunger," I tell him and grab the finger, giving the end a bite.

He stares into my eyes for a second, a second that lasts too long, that reaches into my insides and pulls them apart before putting them together again in a warm symphony that I haven't ever felt before.

Then he pulls his hand back and walks through the door, leaving me with a different type of hunger in need of appeasing.

When I follow him, I'm taken aback by the bright colors that assault me straight away, offering a stark difference to the characterless distillery.

We go through a small hallway that looks like it's being used for storage. One wall is filled with shelves that hold anything from gloves to wine bottles, scissors to seedlings, and everything in between.

From there we come into a big, open space. The staircase is situated on the other end, while an old, dark wooden table and chairs make up a dining room in front of a red-bricked fireplace that's got a few logs in it, keeping the dining area warm.

The fireplace, built in the middle of the room, divides the space in two, the opposite side also has a separate log burning nest facing a cozy living room that consists of a gray, floral-patterned sofa propped against the floor-to-ceiling windows, a leather armchair on either side of the fire, and cute accents in the likes of coffee tables, lampshades, decorative animal statues, and a scatter of books in different places.

"Kitchen is this way," Brody grumbles and points back at the direction of the dining room.

"Sorry," I apologize. "I got distracted."

"And you thought you'd give yourself a tour of my house?" He grimaces.

I shut up and follow him to the other side where the dining room leads to a large kitchen. It's got the same dark-stained wood flooring as the rest of the house, white cupboards, and hazel-colored marble countertops. A large, square kitchen island is in the middle with two chairs on one side.

"You've got a lovely home," I tell him, and I mean it.

I don't usually notice details, nor do I care for decor, but something in Brody's house makes me feel...comfort. I'm both in awe of his space and feel welcome at the same time. Even if its owner doesn't look very happy about my being here.

I expected to find a drab house, dusty surfaces, messy floors, but it's spotless. Which tells me he puts in a lot of work keeping it that way. A house this size doesn't keep itself clean.

Hell, mine in London is a third the size of his, and I have to get help most of the time. But Brody isn't the kind to ask for help. He's barely accepting mine. There's no chance he has a cleaner.

"Thanks," he says. "Knives are there, pots are there."

I nod and set my bag on the kitchen island, and I start taking the stuff I bought out.

"I hope you like risotto," I tell him.

He shrugs and walks to his fridge where he grabs a can of Coke.

"And I wasn't sure if you like red or white, so I brought both." I show him the bottles of wine I bought, but he doesn't bat an eyelid.

"I'm more of a maple wine guy," he says.

Of course. I didn't think of that. *Why didn't I think of that?*

Am I losing my touch? Nothing I do or say seems to impress him or even soften him.

Well, wait until he tries my parmesan pumpkin risotto. He'll crumble right in my hands.

"Ah, of course!" I say, raising a finger in the air. "I thought you might like a change."

"Well, I don't," he says.

"You're a liar," I tell him as I open a cupboard to retrieve a pot. "I saw all the wine you have in the hallway."

He shrugs again.

"They were wedding presents."

I stare at him.

"And that's all people gave you? Wine? What an awful wedding present."

Brody sits down on one of the chairs at the kitchen island and sips his drink.

"It's not when all your friends are farmers or brewers. I've still got a whole keg of IPA somewhere. From one of Theo's relatives."

"Somewhere suggests you've forgotten where it is."

"And?"

"How do you lose a keg of beer?"

He doesn't answer. Instead he watches me chop the onions and turn the gas on for the stove.

Right. No answer to that.

"How did you two meet?" I ask him.

"Our moms are best friends."

"Ouch."

He nods and gulps the rest of his Coke.

"Ouch indeed. Do you need me to help with anything? I might go check on the fire."

He's barely had a second with me in a non-professional capacity and he's already leaving me?

What is going on? Has Logan Graves lost it? What

happened to men swooning over me, begging me to fuck them rough and hard against their kitchen table?

Was Oz right? Am I not Brody's type? Is there a person whose type I'm not? Twenty years of bed-hopping tells me there isn't such a creature.

So why the hell is Brody Mercier resisting me?

Have I lost more than my creativity in the last few months? Have I lost my sex appeal too?

If so, what have I got left?

A house that I own and more than a few pennies in the bank. But is that it?

My career is built on my adventurous sex life, so if I've lost both my writing ability *and* my sexuality, what have I got left?

Who am I without writing and sex?

12

BRODY

Over the following week, Logan inserts himself into my life more and more. Cooking lunch for me becomes a daily occurrence. So much so, that when I put my jeans on this morning, I had to leave the top button undone and the scale tells me I've put on five pounds, which is crazy.

And the worst part is, I actually like it.

I like the way he barges into my kitchen and makes himself at home. I like his cooking. It's tasty and filling in a fuzzy-feeling-in-your-chest kind of way. And my distillery looks empty when he leaves in the evenings and every time I walk into it in the early mornings.

I've never had this before. Someone who not only forces themselves into my life but gets comfy with the role they have in it.

It's not just the confidence he exudes every single one of his waking moments. It's not the good looks and the cocky smirk that I'm so sick of. It's his energy. He's not shy—not by any means—and speaks his mind, like I do. And even though he keeps suggesting he wants more from me, my turning him down doesn't change him. He doesn't go off in a huff or stop talking to me. If anything he becomes even friendlier. Even warmer. Even smilier.

It's crazy to think, but I'm getting addicted to his company. Crazier still because I barely know anything about him. Most of our time is spent on business talk. On branding and identity. On my story and how we can put it out in an appealing way on my website.

Oh yeah, I have a website now. It's almost ready to go live, but Logan wants to have another look at it before we launch it. It's nothing fancy or complicated. Mainly working off an existing template and customizing it to fit my colors, but it's far more than I had before. Hell, he's even convinced me to put a store online, although I don't see a point in a store that only sells one product.

"Just wait until I'm done with you," was his answer when I told him that yesterday.

So, I guess I have no course of action but to wait.

Before I duck into the distillery, I make some fresh pancake batter and whip up a few. Then I stack them on a plate and cover them with aluminum foil to take through to work. It's not long before I hear the roar of another engine outside and the door of the distillery slides open.

Logan walks in with a big box in his hands. It looks heavy because his muscles are flexing and the veins are visible.

Before I can offer my help—I'm too distracted by his big, strong arms—he drops the box by my desk with a thump and stands up straight, taking big breaths that make his chest look even tastier than it does already. The hard nipples peaking under the T-shirt help the overall sexy look too. You know, before I remember I'm not interested.

It's funny, but the more time we spend together, the harder it is to convince myself that's true.

"Aw, did you buy me bricks? You shouldn't have," I tell him, and he raises an eyebrow while wiping his forehead.

"Is that a traditional Vermont gift I should know about?"

"Yes. It's actually considered rude to not take bricks to your host on your fifteenth visit to their house. Didn't anyone warn you?"

I get up and stand next to him, looking down at the box.

"I'll remember for next time," he says.

"So if it isn't bricks…"

"Auden called me this morning," he says. "They managed to finish the labels early, so I picked them up on my way here."

"Why did they call you and not me? Also…labels!" I get down on my knees and open the box faster than the speed of light, feeling the first layer of labels against my hand.

They look even prettier in person, and not only are they more attractive, but they also look like a hundred bucks with their embossed golden elements. I never considered doing anything fancy with my previous branding because… Well, it wasn't the most attractive, and I wouldn't have invested anyway, but Logan…

He knows what he's talking about. Or at least I think he does. I do prefer the new look and direction. I just hope it pays off.

"You know what this means, right?" he tells me.

"What?" I ask, unable to take my eyes off the box.

"That we can go to the farmer's market on Saturday and test out the new look."

"I guess so." I smile at him, and he not only takes notice but also burns me with his icy gaze. So much so that I feel out of breath just looking at him.

"I-I…um, I made you some pancakes," I tell him. "They should still be warm."

"You did?" he asks me, and his smile widens.

He looks at the plate on the desk and uncovers the foil, the doughy scent infiltrating my nostrils.

"I love them with a bit of my wine drizzled, but you could use some of the maple syrup if you want," I tell him.

He sits down and brings the plate in front of him, taking my advice and pouring a bit of maple wine over them. Then he cuts a piece and puts it in his mouth. A mouth I can't stop staring at. The pink lips shrinking and widening as he chews. The wine oozing from the edges of his mouth. The tongue licking over the wet patches and collecting the sweet booze. If only I could lick his mouth clean.

"This is delicious. Strong, but...nice," he says, his eyes pinning me at the last word. We stand there in silence for a few moments, taking in each other's beautiful gazes.

"Come on, Brody. You're better than this," I tell myself, and Logan's gaze drops to my lips.

When is my brain going to learn to filter things properly?

Argh. How embarrassing.

"I'm gonna...I'll go grab some bottles and we can start relabeling."

"Sounds fine by me," he says. "In the meantime, I'll finish off here."

Nice. Thanks for the visual. Now all I can think about as I walk to the pile of crates is Logan over a plate of pancakes, beating off while drenched in maple wine. And me licking him clean.

"You sit tight, you bastard," I order my awakening dick before I grab a crate and take it back to the office area.

"Do you have any brothers or sisters?" Logan asks long after we've started the laborious and boring process of relabeling thousands of bottles.

I can't believe we spent a week rubbing the old ones off. The sheer volume of ice and sponges we'd gone through. The amount of polishing after. No one could have convinced me to do any of that. No one but *this* guy.

I shake my head.

"Any news from Mr. Coggan? That's Theo's last name right?" he asks, rubbing his palm around a wine bottle so suggestively that I could sit and watch him do nothing but that and still come undone.

Fuck!

"No. Why would I?"

He shrugs.

"I just thought… He looked like he wanted you back that day he was here. I thought he might try and get you to hook up again."

The snort that comes out of me is so sudden and loud that I almost drop my bottle.

"Please. That ship has sailed. Like S-A-I-L-E-D, sailed."

"Good." He smirks.

That fucking smirk.

He goes back to his job and I go back to mine.

I don't know why he has to ruin it with talking. Isn't the silence okay? Do we have to speak words just to fill in the void?

When you're forced to speak, you're forced to say things out of necessity. And when you say things out of necessity, you spout things that mean nothing just so there's something *to* say.

And that's when trouble starts. When you say "I love you," but don't mean it. When you promise to always be by someone's side, and yet you're not. When you say there's nothing more important in the world than you, but in fact, there is.

"What happened between you two?" he asks.

"Huh?"

"Theo and you? What went on?"

My face—my body—stiffens, and I can feel my grip around the wine bottle tightening.

"It doesn't concern you," I say.

Logan sighs.

"Okay. But the engagement party is in two days, and I feel like I don't know more about you than anyone else in town."

"And that's a problem because?"

Logan frees his hands and leans over to hold mine.

"I'm just trying to help," he says.

"So you can put on a performance," I tell him.

"It's not just that. I...I like you, Brody. And I can see you're...still hurting. Sometimes talking to someone—especially a stranger—can help you move on," he says and squeezes his hand around mine.

It's warm, and it makes my hairs stand on end. I've never had anyone make me feel so...alive before. Not even Theo during our good times. And if his touch makes me feel this way, I can't even begin to imagine how being with him would make me feel.

Perhaps he's right. Perhaps I do need to open up. Maybe a rebound is all I need, even if I try to deny it. Or maybe it's the months of abstinence that are muddying up my mental clarity.

"Fine," I tell him. "But if I'm gonna do this, I'm not doing it sober."

"Well, I *have* been begging for a tasting so that sounds fine by me," he responds.

I pull my hands away from his and stand up.

"Great. Then maybe we can try to find the blend you made me fuck up that first day," I tell him.

"Will it get us drunk?"

"Yeah, I can get you drunk," I say, only to be met by that smirk again.

I go into the barrel room with jugs in hand and fill three of them up to take to Logan. Then I go back for the other two barrels and return with two more jugs of my golden liquid, but when I try to set them down, there's no space. The desk is filled with bottles and labels and all sorts of garbage from our joined efforts.

"Maybe we should go inside?" I offer, gesturing toward the internal door.

He smiles and picks up the other jugs, then follows me through the distillery into the house and then my living room.

The fire is burning, but before we settle down, I chuck another log in it.

"So how does this work?" he asks when I bring a tray of glasses and set them down in front of us.

"It's simple. We take each wine and mix it with another wine, then we taste it. We can mix three as well. Because each wine has been maturing for a different set of time, in a different cask, it might taste different.

"For my main wine, I use equal parts of one and two. Sometimes, I will use a bit of the others, but one and two always go into every blend. I always mature the wine in them for the same amount of time, so I have some sort of consistency. The others are something I experiment with, but so far, I haven't seen any fascinating results."

"Okay, all I heard was we're mixing drinks, and all I've got to say is, hit me." He bangs a glass on the table in front of him.

I lift a jug of number one and fill his glass with a thumb of maple wine. He knocks it back before I've even filled mine.

"Sorry, I was thirsty," he says, and I refill.

We clink our glasses, and I taste the vanilla-sweetness aging in the first barrel. The one Grandad left me after he passed. One and two have been here since I inherited the farm. I know I'll probably need to replace them at some point in the future, but for now they're doing the job they're meant to. Offering the same sipping comfort of Grandad's original mix.

"All right, for every shot I take, you tell me one thing about you. Deal?" Logan says when I fill up the same glass with equal parts of two and three.

"Only if you tell me something of equal importance too," I say.

He gives me his hand and we shake on it.

This is bound to get interesting.

"You start," he says. "Same question as before."

"What was it again?"

"What happened with you and Theo?"

"Oh," I say and drink a shot. "He decided he still had a life to live. He didn't want to settle down. Was scared we were getting married too fast and needed time to find himself. To find out if he was still in love with me."

"That's a horrible excuse. What a wanker," he says, and I have to laugh at the use of the word.

"Worst part is *he* is the one that proposed. Not me. I was happy to wait."

"So you're not into marriage?" he asks.

I shake my finger between us, and he frowns.

"I've said enough. Your turn now."

"What do you want to know?"

"Let's see. We've spent so much time together, yet I hardly know a thing about you." I pour us a different mix. "How old are you? Where in Britain are you from? And what are you doing here in Vermont?"

Logan leans back and gives me the once-over.

"That's three questions. It's hardly fair considering I only asked you one," he says.

I shrug and down my drink.

"Well, I shared some deep crap. It's the least you can do."

"Fine. I'm forty-two. I'm from London. Born and bred. And I'm here…to find myself," he says.

"See? That wasn't so hard," I tell him. "Now…" I put my hand on his knee without really thinking about it, but I remove it straight away. "Where did you lose yourself? We can go look if you want. Two pairs of eyes are better than one."

Logan helps himself to another blend, and I'm pretty confident this supposed tasting is already going off the rails and will probably need repeating with some actual note-taking another day, but I hardly care right now.

"You're funny," he says in a way that means I'm not. "Okay, my turn again. How many men have you been with?"

I gasp and choke on the sip I just took.

"Are you serious?"

"Very." He smirks and drinks his shot.

"Let me think," I say and start counting on my fingers. "Six. I think."

"Just six?" he asks, the shock visible on his face.

"What's wrong with six?"

He shrugs.

"I don't know. It's a small number. That's all."

"Why? How many have you been with?"

His whole body freezes. I've hit a jackpot here. I can tell.

"Um…a lot more than six," he says when I nudge.

"A lot more is not a number," I say. "I gave you a number."

He looks at me, his eyes all serious, his lip quivering.

"I can't give you a number," he says.

"Oh, come on. That's not fair. Just tell me."

Instead of lightening the mood, his shoulders hunch even more.

"It's not that I don't want to. It's…I don't know," he says, and I've never heard him sound so sad and so sincere at the same time.

"That many?" My voice trembles.

I can't imagine what it's like being him. But I certainly didn't imagine him being so giving with his time and penis.

"If you had to make a number?" I ask, my voice still shaky, so I try and steady it with more wine.

"I...um..."

"Please."

I don't know why I'm begging. Or why I care. But I am and I do. And I want to know.

"Somewhere in the three hundreds?" There's no pride in his words. Or joy. It's just a marbled face and a steady, cool voice. Not the Logan I've come to expect. I even miss the smirk on his face.

"That's...um..." I sigh and drink another shot.

And here I am, picturing this guy in my bed. How can I ever please a guy who's got so much...experience? What would a person like me have to give him?

"Yeah, that's...um..." he says and drinks some more too.

"I mean, I bet it's fun."

I have to say something. Even though it might not be what I really think. He looks sad and dejected enough for the both of us.

"I...I used to think that too," he says and looks at me again, his eyes slitted and pained. "But it's starting to lose its appeal."

"Really? How so?"

"I guess it's the same with anything you do in excess. When you...when you do it so much, with so many, it stops being fun or personal. It starts becoming..."

He pauses and looks at the table. It's already looking wet and sticky, and we've barely even started.

"It becomes what?" I ask him and my hand finds its way to his knee again.

He shakes his head but doesn't look at me.

I lean closer until I get a whiff of his cologne, pungent and spicy, fitting for a man like him.

"It becomes…what?" I ask, my words barely a whisper.

I don't know why I need to know, but I do. It's not like he's a real boyfriend or even a friend. He's a stranger who just happened into my life and changed it significantly without my realizing.

His head drops so he's staring at my vintage carpet when he says the next few words that should make me want to get rid of this man, to dispose of him like he has disposed of over three hundred men. But the sincerity and the guilt in his tone makes me want to hold him closer, to feel his touch, the warmth of his skin on mine.

"It becomes…you just become numb to it. The…guys stop being guys. They become a hole. A hole of momentary pleasure that's so repetitive it even stops being pleasurable. And it's addictive. So addictive that even when it offers no pleasure at all, you have to do it. To feel something, anything other than empty."

"Maybe you need to…" I start but hesitate.

Logan looks up at me, and the movement startles me for some reason. I pull my hand off his knee and rest it on my leg.

"I need to?" he asks.

He sits up the more we breathe, and I'm suddenly aware of how warm it is. His arm is glued to mine. We're sitting close, and it feels even closer with the heat surrounding us.

"Maybe you just need to…" I start and have to stop and clear my throat before I continue. "To change things up. Not positions, I mean. I'm…maybe you just need to approach guys differently. Not sleep with them from the get-go. But get to know them first. Get close to them. Be their friend. Maybe that's how you make the sex part have some sort of meaning again. Because you'd be sharing your soul as well as your body with a friend, not just a lover."

He watches me with red eyes, the muscles on his face tightening at the intensity of this moment, although it could be just me. It feels like he's listening. Like he's really listening to what I'm saying. And I want to offer more to him. More comfort, companionship, or friendship.

But I don't want to be just another lost number in his forgotten tally.

"Yeah," he says. "Maybe I need to do that."

I smile and jump to refill our glasses. He sits back, waiting for me to do so.

We knock back a few more shots, and I have a vague memory of one blend we try that is very appealing to the tongue. But we've had a lot, and I haven't used any palate cleansers, so it's probably just a deceiving tastebud.

And all the time we're getting absolutely wasted, his words circle back in my head. His eyes. The guilt in his voice. The regret. Everything he admitted.

It can't be easy saying those things to a stranger. There must be a story there. A reason why he ended up so addicted and void. Yes, the sheer amount of lovers is intimidating, but the man himself isn't. He can't be. He's big, strong, and handsome, but for the first time since I met him, I see a vulnerability to him that he tries to hide on a daily basis. A vulnerability he probably can't even admit to himself. Yet with a little maple wine and a lot of positive encouragement…

Oh, fuck it. He needs to feel something. And me? I'm already feeling it. I've been resisting long enough. I've been denying my attraction to him since that moment I set eyes on him in Vino and Veritas, because I am hurt and emotionally unavailable. But maybe I can be trusting and open. And if not, maybe I can be another number in his life. Who cares? As long as it helps me move on. And as long as it makes him less empty.

I'm ready to move on. I'm ready to rebound. And who cares about feelings? Maybe Logan thinks feeling momentary pleasure isn't enough to fill the void, but so what? Maybe I just want to feel some pleasure, even if it is meaningless. Feelings are for suckers anyway. I had feelings for Theo, and look where that got me?

I turn around, ready to take his mouth, to relive the kiss we haven't had since the first time we met. My body awakens in anticipation.

Only Logan is lying back on the couch, eyes closed, fast asleep.

I pause and look at the way his body has relaxed. The way his chest rises and falls in rhythm. And I see the peace in his face. No smirk, no cockiness, just himself.

Any disappointment I feel is overpowered by the calm watching him sleep brings me.

"It's better this way," I tell myself as I get up.

I need to move on, I know. But not with him. Not with someone who's used to meaningless. That would only send me down a worse spiral. I approach the armchair next to the fireplace and pick up the blanket that's there, returning to Logan and propping his legs up on the couch.

He shuffles but doesn't wake up, so I cover him with the blanket, I pull the table away from him—I don't know if he's a jerker in his sleep, but better safe than sorry—I add another couple of logs in the fireplace and go upstairs to my own —empty—bed.

"He's just a visitor, Mercier. Don't get attached. Boys like him don't stick around for long," I tell myself as I lay down and succumb to the beauty of a dreamless sleep.

LOGAN

My face is warm and my lips are dry. My throat feels swollen, but the rest of my body is cold.

I open my eyes and am taken aback by the unfamiliar surroundings. I look around me and go through the events of last night, but as soon as I see the shots and jugs of wine on the coffee table it all comes rushing back.

The game I decided to play to loosen his tongue and learn more about him. The sweet booze that has more than just a kick. The questions I asked, thinking I could finally get Brody into bed. My pouring my heart out instead, and showing my true colors to a person for the first time.

After last night, there's no chance I'm going to win this bet, is there?

But maybe Brody is right. Maybe I need to change. Maybe losing the bet might be what my body and soul need to find the missing piece in my life.

After all, I haven't had sex since I started hanging out here, and yet my writing game is stronger than ever. I've written more than ever before in my life. I can hardly contain myself every time I'm home alone. Maybe I don't need sex and adventures to have a career. Maybe I just need Brody in my life, as a friend.

"Morning, lightweight!" Brody says. "How are you feeling?"

His voice... It's like there's a tennis ball inside my head that keeps bouncing from temple to temple, ear to ear, eye to eye.

"I feel like I drank my weight in maple wine," I say.

Brody laughs and crosses his arms. The sound of his laughter makes my hanging head feel close to combustion, yet it also fills my body with warmth. A warmth that travels across all my limbs and fills me with unimaginable energy. Even my dick.

I want this man. God, I want this man. But not just for a night. I couldn't do that to him.

Hell, I couldn't do that to me. Not after last night.

"I hope you're hungry because I have pancakes, bacon, and eggs waiting for you," he says, smiling.

If I wasn't sure I wanted him before, I'm sure now.

"I think I may just love you," I tell him and stand up.

Only it's a bit too fast, so the room starts spinning.

I put my hands out and try to steady the whirlwind in my mind before I follow Brody to the other side of the fireplace where he's laid the table with breakfast. And a large cup of coffee awaits me too.

"Yup. I do love you," I tell him and lift the cup of black heaven to my lips.

I can feel the intensity of his stare on the side of my face even though I've got my eyes shut, enjoying the brew. But when I open them, he seems focused on his own plate of pancakes.

"I thought I'd go a bit Britain-meets-America with breakfast this morning," he says. "Although I wasn't sure if you'd like any maple on anything after last night."

"Is it maple wine or syrup?" I ask.

"Syrup," he says apologetically.

"I think I can manage that," I say and pour some on my pancakes and bacon. I leave the scrambled eggs undressed and instead grind some peppercorn over them.

Each bite is divinity in my mouth. My head becomes clearer and my stomach less whiny.

"I'm sorry about last night," I tell him after a few minutes of eating in complete silence.

A silence that doesn't feel suffocating or expectant.

"What for?"

"For bringing such a foul stop to the evening," I tell him. "I went dark, didn't I?"

Brody holds his cup in his hands and takes a sip before he answers.

"You wanted to know me better, but I got to know you too. There's nothing wrong with that, is there?"

I shake my head and turn back to my food. I don't talk again until I've obliterated the entire thing.

"That was amazing," I tell him. "Make me breakfast like this every day, and I might just marry you."

"Don't make promises you can't keep," he tells me with a chuckle, getting up to clear the plates.

I consider his words for a moment. The meaning behind them.

They're more than just a joke. They're a direct response to what I admitted to him last night. He knows I'm a player, that I don't settle. His joke isn't a coincidence.

And that hurts my stomach, even though I've just filled it with enough bacon and pancakes to last me a week.

I want to tell him I mean it, but I don't want to lie to him. He's right. I don't settle. I don't do relationships.

He comes back after clearing our plates and refills my cup of coffee, and all I can think is no one has done this for me, ever.

It's because you haven't given anyone a chance.

I'm always in for a shag and out the door before they can get out of bed. If we even get as far as their house or bed.

I've not regretted a single thing in my life ever. I've enjoyed —far more than enjoyed—living it. I have liked the excitement of the game, of conquering men. Men who may have been unattainable for poor teenage Logan, but who bend over back-wards—sometimes even literally—for me.

But what I told Brody last night is true. It's lost its appeal. It's become mundane. Knowing I can get anyone. Knowing that whoever I set my eyes on cannot resist me. And while it's fun in theory, I have become detached from it. Even before I bang my current conquest, I think about the next. I barely get more than a second of happiness from each release before I come up with a game plan for the next hole. The next man to become a mindless, arbitrary number in my list.

"Are you okay?" Brody asks me, bringing me out of the foggy haze in my head.

"Yes," I rush to say. "I'm fine."

"Okay. By the way, we need to talk about the dress code for tomorrow," he says.

"For the farmer's market?"

"For the party," he reminds me.

"Of course. The party. Sorry. Head's still spinning. So much for finding out more about each other last night, huh?"

He shrugs.

"I don't know. I thought it was a great evening. I got to

know the real Logan," he says, and I feel like I've been punched in the guts.

Last night he saw a part of me that I never wanted him to see. A part I never show anyone.

"Yeah, but we'll need to know the practical stuff too."

"Like what?" he asks.

"I don't know," I say. "Like how long we've been dating."

"Two months," he says without thinking.

"Or where we met."

"Online," he offers. "We met online, and we've been exclusive since."

I arch an eyebrow and he shrugs.

"What? It happens to so many people nowadays. It's not unusual," he says.

"No. No, it's not."

"What else?" he asks.

We start going through our fake dating history, and the more we expand on it, the more I wish it was how we met. That we were actually a couple. That it wasn't a bet and a stupid challenge that brought me closer to him.

"We covered everything then," he says.

"No-not everything," I tell him.

"What? What's left?"

I don't want to bring it up, but it will make such a difference on whether anyone buys our story.

"There's the physicality thing between us," I say.

"Physicality? What are you talking about?" he stutters, and I see his Adam's apple bob as he swallows.

"We need to look comfortable with each other. As if we spend all our days cuddling and snogging," I tell him. "Making out," I add when I realize he doesn't know what a snog is.

"Oh," he says.

"It's just...the times when we had to do it with Theo, we were very stiff. Which is natural. We didn't know each other then—"

"No, I get it. You're right," he says. "So how do we fix it?"

I get up from the table and focus on him as I walk around.

"We can just hug f-for a moment." I open my arms to him, and he looks at them, hands still crossed over his chest.

I wait for him, watching. Until something flickers in his eyes and he lets go.

He closes the distance between us, and his hands reach up behind my back. We hold each other close. He rests his head on my shoulder, and I rest my cheek on the side of his head.

My hands don't wander. I don't let them. This isn't about winning my bet. It's about giving him what I promised. Making sure his ex doesn't come out the bigger man at this party.

But I don't fail to notice that our bodies fit perfectly. As if they were built for one another.

His breathing synchronizes with mine the longer we stay in the embrace and I feel...I feel home.

"Wh-what next?" he asks, pulling back until he can look into my eyes, but not enough that he escapes our hug.

"Then we kiss?" I say. Because that's all I want to do.

"But...we have kissed before," he mutters.

"Yeah," I whisper. "To show off for Theo. Not...not to show how...desperately in love we are."

"Oh," he says, his breath catching.

I move my head an inch closer to him and wait for his reaction. He doesn't flinch or move back, so I try moving another inch. Still no bite back. But before I can close the gap between us, he does.

Our lips unite in a gentle kiss, and I don't have the guts to deepen it. It's deep enough as it is. It doesn't get closer than this. The ethereal touch of two pairs of lips uniting. Two souls attempting to make something beautiful. Something lasting.

The weight in my chest becomes overbearing and a pin in my heart makes me shudder.

It misses a beat.

And I know with my entire being, even though it has never happened to me in my forty-two years of life, that I have fallen hopelessly in love with Brody Mercier.

BRODY

Logan arrives at seven in the morning the next day—a first for him—and he helps me load my truck.

"Ready?" he asks when we're done.

"Almost. Let me grab the coffee. I made us a thermos," I say and turn to run into the house.

"And pancakes? Please tell me you've made pancakes too," he says behind me, and I can't help the laugh that comes out.

"Wow, Mr. Graves. Demanding much?" I tell him with a grin. "No pancakes...this time."

"You're a cruel boyfriend," he bites back, and I try not to miss a step on my way in.

Boyfriend.

Why does the word coming out of his mouth make me so...?

I wouldn't say hopeful. Or happy. Just...different.

It shouldn't make me feel anything. It's a fake arrangement. That's all we have. One more entanglement in this mess that can't—won't—last past Logan's trip to Vermont.

I mean, he's just a visitor passing by, probably adding more guys to his naughty little list—which he likely doesn't even keep if he doesn't know his number—before moving on to the next destination.

Hell, he probably spends his nights fucking the entire gay population of Burlington. He most likely has a booth at Vino and Veritas and a rotation of men stopping by trying to impress him.

He's not my boyfriend. He's just a man who entered my life all of a sudden and will leave it the same way.

"You bet on it, Mercier," I tell myself as I get the thermos from the kitchen and spot the raspberry brownies on my counter. I grab a Tupperware container and fill it with Mom's goodies before joining Logan outside and jumping behind the wheel.

"Here," I tell him, offering the brownies just as he fills the thermos cup with a splash of coffee. "Courtesy of Mrs. Mercier."

He downs the coffee as soon as he sees the contents of the see-through box.

"Fuck. Hot. Shit. Hot. Fuck. Bollocks," he hisses and reaches for the small bottle of water in the cup holder.

I keep watch of his antics in the passenger seat and set off for Burlington and the farmer's market. We should be there by eight, which leaves us just enough time to set up before the foot traffic starts. Not that it usually makes a difference. I just hope today is better.

"Remind me to give Mrs. Mercier my compliments tonight," he says after his first bite of brownie.

"She doesn't need any more compliments. Trust me. She gets enough as it is," I say.

I feel his gaze on the side of my face, so I appease his curiosity.

"She has a bakery in Fairfax."

"And you only tell me now? Why haven't I been introduced to her baked goods yet?"

He tries to act all incensed, but it doesn't last long, and I dismiss it anyway.

"I'll be sure to make up for that crime from now on," I tell him.

"You better," he rasps, and it sounds like the kind of naughty threat you want to succumb to.

Or not. Because I'm an adult man in full control of his emotions and impulses.

It takes us half an hour to get to Church Street, and as we move stuff from the parking lot to the square, Logan carries a bag of his own.

"What is that?" I ask him.

"Just some stuff to spruce up the display," he says, but he doesn't elaborate any further.

We get everything to my spot, where we set up the tent and table, and it's only when I take a white sheet out to cover the table that he reveals the contents of his bag.

"I thought since we've gone for black and gold with the new branding..." he starts and pulls a black cloth from the bag.

It's smooth and velvety and when the table is all laid out, it looks majestic.

"And I've got a few boxes," he adds, pulling out three wooden crates that fit a bottle each and are filled with golden shredded paper.

When we're done setting up, I barely even remember what my old stall used to look like. All I'm seeing now is an elegant, mysterious, and sexy display of golden sin. Compared to the other displays around us, ours stands out the most with its arcane look.

"Okay, if I don't sell anything now, then I don't know if I ever will."

He arches an eyebrow, hands in his back pockets, and I feel...out of breath.

"That's not the attitude. You *will* sell," he says. "You will sell out."

I rasp my lips and go to stand behind the counter.

"Not 'Pfft.' Say it. *I will sell out.*"

"Are you serious?"

"Absolutely," he replies. "Say it."

"I will sell out," I mumble.

"Great. Now take the conviction to one hundred."

"I will sell out," I say.

"One thousand?" he requests.

"I *will* sell out!" I yell, and some of the market's visitors turn to look at us.

We both burst into laughter as I shout it again under Logan's instructions.

"Fabulous, darling. One more thing," he says as he sets up the stall with small plastic cups. "For tasting," he says at my curious look. "You can't expect people to buy blind. You lure them with the look, you reel them in with the taste. Now for that last missing thing?"

I stare at him and wait, but he doesn't say anything.

Instead he draws a forefinger across his lips, forming a smile. I roll my eyes.

"I smile."

"Internally maybe." He laughs. "But how about we show the world what a beautiful smile you have?"

He thinks I have a beautiful smile? Does he actually mean it, or is he trying to get me to be a better salesman?

And why does his compliment make me feel all fuzzy inside? I bet he says that to all the boys. I'm not special.

Yet, I smile as the first customers approach and when the next ones come through. Traffic is slow at first, but the more people have a taste of the wine, the more people gather, until I find myself doing a whole spiel about the maple wine process and what makes my blend different from your usual home-made fermented maple syrup.

So, naturally, I sell a few bottles. Logan even offers a buy two get one free to those most impressed.

"Get them hooked on the good stuff, and they'll be begging for more," he explains and, of course, I roll with it.

By two o'clock, I'm sold out, and my cheeks hurt from all the smiling and laughing. It turns out I can do small talk with people. Who the hell knew? I always sucked at it before.

As we pack up—an easier job when you have no bottles to carry—I watch Logan and the amount of care he takes with every piece he puts away. The shredded paper gets rescued and put back in the boxes. The sheet folded nice and carefully. And I'm still smiling, even though I'm not selling to anyone.

What has he done to me? What kind of magic? What has he made me?

"Hey," he says when everything is back in the car. "Are you okay?"

"Huh? Yeah, I'm fine."

We head back toward home. It's funny how comfortable I feel with him in my car, my distillery, my house. In a not so funny way. We've only known each other for two weeks, and yet I'm used to his energy around me. I've never been like this with anyone before. Not even with Theo. It took me a few months before I was comfortable sharing everything with him. But once I did, we jumped stages faster than the speed of light.

What on earth had possessed me to say yes to Theo's proposal? I can't comprehend it now, thinking back.

We're back by four, and we immediately start getting ready

for the party. I show him to one of the guest rooms so he can take a shower and get dressed, and I do the same in my room, all the while trying really hard not to think of how naked he must be in only the next room over.

At five we get to Amy Norwich's house, and just before we walk through the front door, Logan stops and stands in front of me, looking into my eyes.

"Everything okay?" I ask him.

"Yeah," he says, fixing my collar that I didn't realize needed fixing.

But I let him do whatever he wants to me. I have no willpower to stop him. Just having those fingers on my neck, his arms at such close proximity, his mouth a breath away, renders me weak.

It reminds me of the kiss we shared yesterday morning. When we were supposed to be practicing for today. And how I wished we could practice every day for the rest of our lives.

There's no rest of our lives, Mercier. We tried that once, remember? With a far less sluttier man, nonetheless.

"How do I look?" I ask him when he takes a step back.

"Perfect," he smiles. And it's an actual smile. Not the cocky smirk he's been treating me to since we met.

I open my mouth to answer him, but what do you say to that? Is there a sufficient response?

"Brody?" someone says behind me, and I fall back to reality instead of whatever dreamworld there is where Logan and I work as a couple.

I turn around and find a pampered Mom and Dad staring at us.

"Hey, Mom. Dad," I tell them.

Logan comes to stand right next to me, and my parents look at him as he puts his hand around the small of my back.

And for the first time since we came up with this devious plan, I realize I never even prepared them for this.

"Who would this be?" Mom asks, her eyes flaring and her hand resting on her collar.

"Logan Graves, pleased to meet you," he says and gives them his hand. "You must be the sinful creator of those raspberry brownies."

Mom's jaw drops, and she shakes his hand, stumbling on her words.

"And you must be Mr. Mercier."

"Indeed," Dad replies. "But you are?"

"Oh," I shudder back to life and fumble to find my words again. "Logan is my...my boyfriend."

Mom and Dad stare at each other and then at me.

"Boyfriend? Since when do you have a boyfriend?" she asks.

"We met online a couple of months ago," Logan says. "We thought we'd take it slow now that I'm in town while we got to know each other better, so it's not his fault. We both kept it on the DL. Isn't that what you say here?"

"Yes. Yes," Mom mutters, still ogling at Logan.

"It's still quite fresh," I add. "I didn't want to tell you anything, especially after what happened with..."

"Oh, honey, nonsense. You don't need to explain," Mom says as if she's suddenly come to life, and she waves me off. "I'm so happy you've found someone. Now, let's not spend the rest of the party standing here. I need a drink, and I need to know *everything*."

So we join the party. And Mom drapes herself all over Logan, finding out everything about him. Things I didn't even know. Like the fact that he's a writer. I didn't know that. Why wouldn't he tell me that?

She also finds out he's been helping me at the distillery, and he so proudly tells her how great I was today at the farmer's market.

Before long, there's a group of people around us, and he recounts his trips around the world and all the mishaps he's had, like lost luggage, sharing an apartment with a nudist by accident, getting food poisoning on a red-eye flight.

His stories are countless, and each gets a different sort of response from the little audience he's gathered around us. I feel like a groupie, the way I'm draped by his side, pretending I'm in love and just as mesmerized.

Although I am. Mesmerized that is. By everything he's experienced. I'm envious of his trips and the people he's met. Of all the things he seems to have done which I've never even aspired to do or ever thought I'd want.

The drinks keep on coming, and it's only when the barbeque is all laid out that the guests disperse and we're free to enjoy our evening.

"Are you this popular at all the parties?" I ask him.

He shrugs.

"I don't usually go to parties like this," he says. "It's nice. Do you think people have bought our...?"

"Our charade? It seems so," I tell him.

"Good. I'm glad," he says.

He excuses himself to the bathroom, and I sit at one of the scattered tables, watching the other guests going about their merry business.

"He's gorgeous," Mom says, coming to sit beside me. "Charismatic."

"Yeah," I mumble and fill my mouth.

I can't lie to her any more than I have already. I didn't expect everyone to like him so much, especially not my parents, which makes this charade feel dirty now. I just want this party to be over.

"And best of all, he makes you smile," she says, patting my knee.

"I smiled before him."

I don't mean to whine, but it comes as such regardless of my intent.

"No, sweetheart. You didn't. You haven't in a long time," she says, and her gaze flicks behind me.

Her warm, affectionate face hardens. I turn to look at what caused the change and find none other than Theo and his new sugarmaker walking through the door to the backyard.

"I can't believe he showed up," Mom curses.

"Wait, isn't this why you wanted me to come to the party? To save face?"

"Well, I wasn't sure he'd show. I was just trying to get you out of the house. But if I'd known the kind of hunk you were hiding there, I wouldn't have bothered."

"Mom!" I grimace. "Don't be gross."

"Why? What did I say?" she asks, all innocent.

Theo stands to the side with Skyler and scans the backyard just as Logan comes out from the house.

"Logan, yoo-hoo," Mom jumps in her seat and waves at him.

I glare at her.

"What?" she asks.

"Yoo-hoo? Since when do you 'yoo-hoo?'"

She turns her attention behind me again and puckers her lips.

"Since you have a sexy man to show off in front of your ex-fiancé," she says, and when Logan approaches, she stands up and drapes herself all over him.

I get up from my chair and mouth an apology to him. He smirks and answers Mom's questions. Theo's staring. Of course he is. While his "special friend" is talking to him.

"Excuse me, Harper. Would you mind if I ask your son for a dance?" Logan asks when he notices me staring behind him.

"But-but there's no music," she says.

"That's never stopped me before," he replies and gives me his hand.

I let him pull me closer to him. Mom all but faints watching us in the tight embrace. And Theo is probably staring. Everyone is most likely staring as we sway side to side like two crazy people.

Two crazy people in love.

I know it's all for show, but it feels good being looked after like this. Being the center of someone's attention. Having someone like him by my side, doing all the impressing and socializing I don't care much for. Being envied for having bagged such a treasure of a man.

We keep on dancing, and eventually someone puts music on, and more couples join in on the dancing. But Theo and Skyler aren't dancing. My ex is too busy staring. And Skyler keeps occupied by talking to Amy's grandmother.

By the time the party's over—a decided blast thanks to Logan, according to everyone—I've almost convinced myself our little charade is real. Everyone else certainly believed it.

"I would say tonight was a success," he says when he walks me to my front door like any gentleman would.

I never knew I had a thing for gentlemen until now. Maybe it is a little emasculating, but it still fills my stomach with butterflies.

"Yes. I think it was," I tell him. "I bet you're glad it's all done now."

He grimaces.

"What makes you say that?"

"Well," I say and unlock my door. "You only have one

more day next week to pretend you're my boyfriend. I bet it's not good for your reputation to appear tied down."

I turn the latch and swing my door open, too scared to look at him and face the truth in my words.

"Is-is that what you think of me?" he asks.

His voice sounds pained, and I forget my fear for a moment and turn to face him.

His eyes are slits staring into my own, his shoulders hunched, his hands in the pockets of his jacket.

"Well…you like adventure, don't you? In the bedroom and out of it? It must be boring hanging out with the same guy for—"

"Is that how little you think of me?" he asks. "After everything I shared with you on Thursday?"

"I don't…I…"

My words have abandoned me. I don't even know what I'm trying to say, let alone how to make it sound any less insulting.

"I just mean… I don't know. You're an adventurer. You've been with more guys than I could ever have in five lifetimes. There's nothing Brody Mercier could offer you that you haven't experienced already."

"How can you be so sure of that?" he asks, taking a step closer to me.

I keep my gaze on his chest. I can't look him in the eyes. His focus is too penetrating. Too tempting. And I'm already being stupid. I don't need to do anything more monumentally embarrassing.

"Because. I'm a nobody. I'm just a sugarmaker who talks to himself and can't sell a thing without someone's help. What could I possibly give you that you don't already have?"

My heart?

No, I can't give him that. It's already had enough heartbreak as it is. But then again, it's in pieces anyway, so why not?

It's not worth much anyway, but I would give it to him if he were willing to take it. However, I'm just a hole. Not even a hole actually. I'm just an acquaintance. A blip in his long and exciting life.

Logan takes another step forward, and my eyes are forced to look up at him as he's only inches away.

"What do you think I have?" he rumbles.

"E-everything," I reply.

His throat tightens and his Adam's apple moves before he speaks.

"You're wrong," he says. "I don't have *you*."

I pause, trying to comprehend what he's saying.

He wants me? Why? Since when? How?

It doesn't matter now. I want him. He wants me, or so he says. What have I got to lose?

"Then have me," I tell him.

He doesn't need to be told twice. His hands come flying out of his pockets and grab my face, closing what little distance we have with his mouth.

We collide, and I zing with the energy he gives off. His lips, his hands, his breath. They all seem to feed him with more of it.

He takes a step forward, and I'm forced to take a step back. We keep going until we stumble into the dining room.

Logan grabs the chair from behind me and throws it away from us before he lowers me to the table until we're both lying on it.

I put my hands around his waist and press him close to me while he unbuttons my shirt.

When he parts the fabric from my chest, he trails down, tracing kisses along the middle of my chest, my stomach, stopping at my groin before returning to my mouth, tasting me again and letting me taste him.

I bury my fingers in his hair and grip. A rumble erupts out of him sending blasts of heat across my body. My dick hardens even more. Logan grips my cock and gives it a squeeze before slipping his hand under my waistband.

His touch sears a knot in my stomach. His fingers wrap around my dick. His palm rubbing along my crown.

I haven't been touched like this in five months, and even then it was a quickie to get my quota of sex for the month.

Logan isn't just filling a need. Where he touches, he causes impact. Each move is careful and meticulous as he is. Nothing happens by chance. Not the way his tongue explores my mouth or the feel of his body covering mine.

When he pulls back a few inches and looks into my eyes, I can see the raw need in them. The pure passion.

He wants me.

And I want him.

So I let myself go. For one night we can have each other, even if that's all it ever is.

15

LOGAN

His length pulses in my hand. His body vibrates under me with every move. He yearns for me. He craves me. After so many days, he finally seems to feel just like I have since the moment I set my eyes on him.

It's been a long time coming, and my body could explode from the sheer need I've bottled up in an effort to win him over.

Yet I wouldn't have it any other way. If I'd had him that first day, I would have already moved on. I wouldn't have had the chance to get to know him better; to see the Brody underneath the frown and the heartache.

I move down his body again, only this time I don't stop when I get to his happy trail. Instead I unbutton his jeans and lift his underwear over his cock.

It's long and circumcised, bushy pubes that reach out on the side of his length like little sideburns. He smells sweet, and his slit is leaking precum that I bet my fucking life tastes better than any maple extract in the world.

He massages my head, handfuls of locks between his

fingers, and that urges me on until I take him in my mouth and taste the essence of him.

He shudders with each stroke. My tongue rests on the underside of his cock, and he twitches. His precum wets my palate driving me over the edge.

I've never wanted anyone as much as I want him.

I don't know what it is. If it's how much he's been playing hard to get. If it's his nerdy maple knowledge, or the way he thinks he's smiling when he's frowning.

Or maybe it's how soft his hand is when he holds mine, as if he's unsure of the appropriate pressure required for a fake relationship.

Then there's also the way he licks his lips after every drop of maple wine he tastes.

How he pretends he doesn't care about me but makes sure to check my tires before I set off for Burlington every evening.

Or how he watches me when he thinks I'm not paying attention.

It might be something else entirely. Or it might be all of them together. But if I know anything, it's how deeply I want to be with him.

And not to conquer the inspiration for the next bestseller. Or to win the bet with the bartender. It's not even to quench my thirst for release.

It's because I want—I need—him to make me feel just the way he's made me feel every single day I've known him, and even stronger.

It's not his sex I'm addicted to. It's his presence.

He moans, and the vibration moves all the way to his cock and the back of my throat, and I release him before he lets go. This can't be over. Not yet. Not so soon after it's started.

"Do you want to move this to the bedroom?" I ask him,

and he doesn't respond. He sits up on the table and puts his hands around my neck giving me a wet, promising kiss.

I lift him off the table, and he wraps his legs around my hips. I carry him over to the stairs and take them one by one until we're safely on the second floor, and then he jumps off me, leading me all the way to his bedroom.

He pushes me on the bed but stays standing, pulling one shoulder free of his shirt and then the other. Next, his jeans drop to the floor as do his pants until he's standing there, young, sexy and naked.

I've pictured this moment many-a-night in the comfort of my flat, but nothing beats the real deal.

Especially when he leans over and begins undressing me.

My clothes become another bundle on the bedroom floor, but then his lips wrap around my cock, and I fall back, forgetting my name, my address, my whole existence.

He goes down on me, pulling my foreskin all the way back, and lathers my crown with his tongue.

I may have had three hundred, five hundred, a thousand men, however many there have been, but I've never been sucked like this. I've never been made to feel like this. Like a person. Like more than a dick on a handsome face.

I'm usually inside the guy already by this point, but I don't want to rush this. Not with him. Not with Brody.

He lifts his head and looks up at me, stroking me at the same time.

It's torture. Torture wanting him so badly and wanting to last longer, to be with him all night long. All day long. All week long. Is this what love is like? Wanting to be with the same person for as long as possible? Unable to think straight when you're without them, or even when you're with them?

Is it love when all you want is to take care of them, wipe

away their sadness, hug away their fears, or protect them from any form of harm?

Brody climbs on top of me and kisses his way to my mouth, where our tongues lock in a tight match for dominance.

I'm not surprised. He's a feisty guy in life, it only makes sense he'd be feisty and dominant in bed. I'm usually clear on who's got control of the situation, of who dictates the pace and order of events. It's me. Always me. But with him, with Brody? I let him take control.

He grinds against me, our cocks rubbing together, the friction of our bodies causing sparks to flutter inside me. I let him own more of my mouth while there's a war of shivers all over me.

His hand slides down and grips us both. He gives us a few tugs, and then he moves my cock under him and lowers his arse until my dick is trapped between his cheeks, teased by his hole.

He works his hips along mine, his cock rubbing on my groin making my own cock tense with desire. It's nothing, yet it's so erotic, so intoxicating that it's hard to breathe.

Brody pulls his mouth back and licks along my jawline until he gets to my neck. He bites down on me gently, but also not. Like a vampire feeding on his prey and keeps up the pace of our not-fucking that still makes me feel like Mount Vesuvius —full and so close to eruption.

"Fuck!" I groan, not even realizing it until I hear my voice in the otherwise silent room.

"Mmmm," Brody moans on my neck and sits up to look at me. "Sure, why not," he says and dismounts me, reaching for his bedside table and opening the drawer. "Fuck," he says. "No condoms."

He lifts a bottle of lube from the drawer with a grimace, and a huff comes out of me.

"Don't care. I'm negative," I tell him.

"Really?" he asks, his eyes unreadable slits in the dark.

"Yeah. I never fuck raw," I tell him.

He bites his lower lip, still watching me.

"What?" I ask.

"So I'd be your first?" he says with a little more tease than I've heard him use before.

"You're definitely a first of all kinds."

"What is that supposed to mean?" he asks. "No. Never mind. I don't think I want to know."

He jumps next to me, bottle of lube in one hand, the other tracing patterns on my stomach, his lips finding solace back in mine.

We stay there for what feels like forever, working up to something I don't want to rush, to something I want to take full joy in because I don't know if I'll ever get another chance.

I feel him move the bottle from one hand to the other and he squirts some on his fingers.

And then he goes and places those damn fingers between my legs, the coolness of the liquid making my rim spasm at the surprise.

"What are you doing?" I ask him.

Brody pulls back and frowns.

"What does it look like I'm doing? I'm prepping you," he says.

"Um…why?" I ask him.

"So I can fuck you. Why else?"

"Wait! *You* are fucking *me*?"

Brody sits back and glares at me.

"Yeah. What? You thought because I'm smaller that you get to fuck me?"

"Erm…no. But I…"

"What? You've fallen into the mind trap of mainstream porn that big equals top? Well, I'm sorry to burst your bubble, but I'm versatile. You aren't?"

"Um…I haven't bottomed in a long time," I tell him.

He pouts and looks at me with bloody pity. Pity!

"What a sad life," he says. "I mean, I can bottom if it's such a problem, but—"

"It's not," I say.

It isn't?

"I just…you took me by surprise. That's all."

"So…"

"Let's do this," I tell him, surprising even myself with my eagerness. "Fuck me."

"I thought you'd never ask," Brody answers and attacks my mouth again.

This time it's me who takes our cocks in my hand and strokes them until we're both hard again.

Brody uses more lube on my hole and gets me all wet and stretched, adding one finger at a time. He pushes in and out until I feel the pounding on my prostate, and I can barely contain myself.

When did I get so convinced bottoming was not for me? Why have I denied myself this feeling for so long?

Just as I get used to his fingers inside me, he removes them and replaces them with his crown. I fist the sheets under me on either side and take a deep breath, looking into Brody's dark eyes. His lips part as he feels the pleasure I'm all too familiar with and his heat inside me sends me into all kinds of spirals.

I groan in pain. I moan in pleasure. I gasp in need.

Fuck the fingers. Why haven't I had a dick in me all this time? Had I let myself be convinced that somehow topping is more authoritative, more controlling, more pleasurable? Or have I truly not been fucked so well and good until now?

Whatever it is, I let it go and focus on the moment I opened up to this guy, this bloody guy with his frown and his attitude problems that has the sweetest soul of anyone I've ever met. And the hardest dick I could have asked for.

"Fuck me, Brody Mercier," I tell him, pulling him down to my mouth until we're connected on both ends. "Fuck me until the end of time."

And Brody delivers. He fucks me harder, gentler, rougher until his body trembles against mine and I feel his load in me. And that makes me shoot my load between us. And we're there until early morning. A wet, hot mess.

And there's nowhere else I'd rather be.

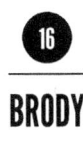

BRODY

The night is long and our adventures under the covers last for most of it.

I resist him the whole night until I finally succumb and let him take me too. Multiple times.

As soon as he's in me I know—I know—I'm in love with him and I don't want this to ever stop. I'm hooked on his smile, his body, his cock, his beauty, and everything in between.

He's insatiable, and I love every second of it. And yet, when he fucks me, he's not rough, he's tender. He knows he's packing, and the sting is real, so he takes it slow and steady, building up a rhythm that weakens me every time he hits my prostate, yet empowers me every time he slides out of me.

His palm rests on my neck, and his eyes? His eyes never leave me. He gazes into me, barely blinking, and I know I have his full attention. I'm the most important person to him right this moment and nothing can distract him from giving it to me, offering me more pleasure, more joy than I've ever had.

Sex with Theo was never like this. It wasn't bad, per se, but it was never so…stimulating and romantic as sex with Logan.

It's quite ironic actually. You'd expect the man with the unquenchable thirst for ass to be a machine, but he's wildly erotic. Tender. Nothing like I ever expected him to be.

A couple of months ago, hell, a few days ago, I would never have thought I'd want sex again, or that I'd ever find sex this good. Or that I deserved anyone like Logan.

And I know—I know—it's so presumptuous of me to assume I deserve Logan, but I can't help it.

I know he's just a fuck. Someone I get to have only once and never again, leaving me only with the fading memory of our time together.

But for a moment, staring into his bright-blue eyes that are steeped with yearning, I allow myself to imagine, what if…

What if Logan was mine? Now and for the rest of my life. What if I was the one that made him settle down? Gave him roots? A place to call home?

"Harder," I tell him, squeezing his face between my hands.

"What?" he asks, a bit of confusion crossing his eyes.

"Harder. Fuck me harder," I command.

It's the only thing I can think of to make me stop imagining a happily-ever-after with him.

The only method I can come up with to distract my brain from his dreamy qualities and his cuteness factor, or how I could get used to that cocky smirk I use to loathe.

By asking him to make it faster and dirtier. This is edging on lovemaking territory, and I don't need that right now. My mind doesn't need that. It needs sex. Rough and naughty sex. I can't cope with more rejection. I don't want any more rejection.

I'm not the one to make a guy like Logan settle down. I couldn't even make Theo, average-boy-next-door Theo, settle down. I'm not going to make this god of a man move to Small Town, Vermont and dream of maple wine, children, and a less-than-average farm life.

"Oh…okay," he replies, and he pounds me just as I asked, slamming his thick manhood into me so hard that I let out a yelp.

And he helps me drown the ache with his mouth and his eager tongue, happy to swallow it and replace it with his sunshine disposition.

"Tell me if you want me to stop," he whispers when he comes up for air, and I feel my entire body is about to give in under the pressure of his weight and his thick meat.

"No," I cry. "Don't stop. Breed me, Logan. Keep going. Give me all you have before it's too late."

My voice breaks. How embarrassing. How needy of me. To be so desperate for him when I hardly know him. When he's not even gonna be in my life next month.

"Whatever you need, baby," he breathes on me. "Whatever you need."

He attacks my mouth yet again, and I squeeze my legs tighter around his hips as he feeds me more of his length. He keeps going until the tension and power in his body loosens, and he obeys my command, filling me up with all he's got.

His face drops to the crook between my head and shoulder, his lips ghostly on my neck, his breath hot and heavy on my skin. He bucks his hips one more time, and I wrap my arms around him until my concerns become a blur and all I care about again is giving him shelter in my embrace.

So much for rough and dirty quenching down the hopelessness. I still want him. I still want *just* him. And I still can't imagine my life without him in it anymore.

I turn my body, and he lies down next to me, his dick slipping out of me, his hot seed spilling out of me. He closes his eyes and cozies up to my chest until he's fast asleep.

But I can't sleep. I'm too conscious, too aware that this is just the start of me getting hurt again and that everything, all the defenses I've ever put up, have been for nothing.

"Stupid, Brody," I scold myself.

I've gone and gotten myself too attached to a stranger. A stranger I know very little about.

Why can't I enjoy a night of hot, raw passion without screwing it all up? Why can't a good fucking be just that? A good—mind-blowing, even—fucking?

I reach for my phone with him still in my arms and Google search the name of the man next to me. I want to know more about him. To convince myself he's no good. To prove to myself that I'm jumping ahead and making something out of nothing. Bringing up feelings where there should never be any.

The first search result is his own website. I click on it, and I'm greeted by a white background, golden calligraphic letters spelling out his name, and underneath, in bold black letters, are the words "author of mostly-true erotic adventures."

"Mostly true?" I ask myself and click on his *About Me* page to find out more about his work.

Until the party last night, I didn't realize he was a published author. I assumed he was on a paid vacation trying to write a book.

How is it possible to feel like you both know and don't know the person sleeping next to you? It's like, I know who he is—helpful, kind, patient—but I don't *know* him. I don't know where he lives or how he grew up, or if he's in an open relationship, or if everything he's told me, everything he presents is entirely fictional.

His picture is front and center on the page, and I scroll down to answer some of my questions. And I realize what kind of man he really is.

He's written over thirty books based on his sexual adventures from city to city, country to country, man to man. That explains his high number of lovers.

He goes, he conquers the hole, he moves on.

"See? No future with a man like him."

Logan stirs next to me, and I click the lock button on my phone and look at him. But he doesn't wake up. He smiles and readjusts his head on the pillow.

God, he's so gorgeous. And I've gone and fallen in love with him, even though I never meant to.

That wasn't part of our deal, was it now?

LOGAN

"So...how is it going? Have you lost the bet yet?" Oz asks as he makes me my morning coffee on Monday.

When I woke up in Brody's arms yesterday, I didn't want to leave. I didn't want to open my eyes or move away from the bed.

Somehow, Brody Mercier has managed to wind himself into my heart, and I have no idea what to do with the realization. Or how I can even do something when my intentions didn't start innocently at all.

"Can we not talk about this?" I ask him.

"Why? Have you given up on trying to fuck the wine guy? See, I told you he wasn't easy like the guys you're used to, but you wouldn't listen," Oz says and passes me the cup I need to wake up.

"Oz, I..."

What do I say? That he's right? That Brody wasn't—isn't— easy? That I haven't just gone and fallen in love with the man, even though I've technically won the bet?

So what if I have. The only person I ever want to sleep with is Brody, and yet the way he reacted to me the rest of the day yesterday, made me think he doesn't feel the same way.

He made me breakfast and he still checked my tires before I came back home, but he pretended as if our night never happened. As if we hadn't been inside each other.

Maybe it isn't a big deal for him, but it is for me. Because no matter what and who I've been through, and regardless of the naughty things I write in my books, I've never let anyone breed me. And I've never bred anyone. I've always done it to protect myself more than anything, but I always also thought that when and if I ever did, it would be with someone special. Not that I ever met them.

Until Brody, of course.

"You're right," I tell Oz. "He's not easy."

"And? Are you giving up?" Oz asks.

I stare at my coffee instead of him. I don't want to lie to him, but then again I barely know him, so why would I tell him the truth?

"Yeah. I guess so," I sigh.

I can feel Oz's intense gaze on me, and I don't know what to do. So I drink the coffee he's made me.

"Are you okay?" he asks. "You don't look... Oh God!"

"What?" I look up at him.

"Oh God," he repeats.

He's looking at me all wide-eyed and speechless, and it's not until I wave a hand in front of him that he speaks again.

"You've fallen in love with him, haven't you?" he asks.

My shoulders arch back and my breath catches.

"How do you know?"

"Oh crap. You have. I was hoping I was wrong," he says.

"Why?"

Oz leans against the coffee machine and crosses his arms,

his eyes hardening when he speaks to me, as if he's a stranger and not a somewhat-friendly face in this town.

"Brody has been through a lot. He doesn't need someone who will take his heart and wretch it out of him without a second thought," he says.

"I wouldn't," I say.

"Are you really in love with him, or do you *think* you're in love with him?"

"Is there a difference?" I ask.

Oz huffs at me.

"I think there is. I've never been in love, but…yes, I believe there *is* a difference. The first one means you're ready to risk everything you have, everything you are for him. The second means you're going to use him until you get bored and move on to the next adventure," he says.

"Adventure? You think this is about my bloody book? I know what I'm feeling, Oz. I'm feeling like I've never felt before," I say.

"But are you ready to give it all up for him? Falling in love means allowing yourself to change, to grow so you can be with someone else. Will you?"

I don't know what he expects of me. I don't even know what to do with my feelings. Whatever I think or feel is irrelevant if Brody doesn't feel the same way.

"I…I think so," I tell him and in response he raises an eyebrow. "I will."

Oz relaxes and a smile appears back on his face.

"Oh good. See, Brody doesn't have an older brother, so I had to make sure someone spoke to you like he would," he explains.

Even though his reaction was scaring me a minute ago, it now makes me feel all fuzzy inside.

"That's sweet of you," I tell him.

"Well, I am mighty sweet if I may say so myself," he replies with a proud smile. Then his smile sinks when he looks behind me. "Oh, hey, Theo," he says.

Shit. How long has he been standing there? Please tell me he just walked in.

I turn around and see the man that broke Brody's heart looking smug and superior staring down at me.

Fuck!

"Can I have a latte to go?" he asks Oz, and Oz gets on it straight away.

"You'd think I was a full-time barista and not a stockroom assistant with all these coffees I'm making," he mumbles to himself, for our benefit entirely.

"Is there a problem?" I ask Theo when he won't stop staring.

"No. No problem at all," he replies. "No problem *at all.*"

Yet he insists on staring.

"Whatever you think you heard is wrong," I tell him. As if that's going to accomplish anything.

"Oh, I don't *think* I heard anything," he says.

Oz hands him his coffee in a to-go cup, and Theo hands him a five-dollar bill and strides away.

He may have heard everything, or he might pretend he knows more just to make me feel uncomfortable. Just to take advantage of my weakness. But regardless, I know my time with Brody is limited. One way or another, this bubble is going to burst, and there's nothing I can do to stop it. I wouldn't even know how.

"Hello, darling," Chloe says when I answer the phone.

The flat is cold and dark when I get in after my morning at

Vino and Veritas. I was on my way to pick up my laptop before I head to Brody's farm when my phone rang.

"You know what I'm going to ask," she says when I respond to her greeting.

I sit down at the dining table and open the document on my laptop. I want to reassure her. I want to tell her everything is going well. And it is. In theory.

"Well, I've got twenty-four thousand words so far, so halfway through," I tell her.

"Oh, excellent," she says as I read the last line on my manuscript so far.

I loved him. Loved him more than words could ever express.

Isn't that the truth?

"Although, I have a slight issue," I tell her.

"Okay. I'm listening. Whatever it is, I'm sure we can fix it," she says.

I rub my forehead and think twice before I tell her. For all I know, my career is over.

"It's not erotic fiction," I tell her.

"What isn't?" she asks.

"The book. The one I'm writing? What else are we talking about?"

"Then what is it?"

"It's...it's a romance," I tell her.

"Oh. Okay. That's not bad then. I thought you were going to tell me it's prose, or worse, literary fiction," she laughs. "Romance we can work with."

"We can?" I ask her.

"Of course we can. You just need some of your signature steamy scenes, and we'll have a brand-new Logan Graves erotic romance."

I bite my lip and chew on it while Chloe goes silent on the other side.

"What is it?" she asks after a few seconds.

"Nothing. Um…it's just…how bad would it be if I didn't?" I ask. "Add the steamy scenes, I mean."

"Are you trying to tell me you wrote a sweet romance? You?"

I shrug, even though I know she can't see me. "No. Maybe. I don't know," I tell her. "This book means a lot to me. I don't want it to be like everything else. This book is different."

"Well, okay, darling. But your brand is erotic fiction. Are you trying to tell me you want to change?"

"I don't know," I sigh. "Maybe."

"Hmmm…not the end of the world, I guess. I'll tell you what. Why don't you finish what you have, and then we'll see what we're working with? Worse case, they reject it and give you a new deadline."

"They won't give me another chance," I tell her.

It's become clearer in the last year or so. If I fail to deliver again, they'll probably move on to the next person who can write what I write. Hell, they'll probably hire a ghostwriter to continue the Logan Graves literary legacy. If you can call it that.

"You don't know that. Maybe if they see you can still write, that you can still deliver, they'll change their minds. But you have to finish it, all right? Or I'll make you pay," she says, and after I agree with a chuckle I don't even feel on my throat, let alone in the rest of my body, she hangs up.

It's different. This one's different. I keep telling myself.

Now I just have to convince him he actually is. And convince him to take a chance on me.

BRODY

"A brand is a whole package," Logan says to me, sitting across my office desk at the distillery, acting as if nothing happened between us. Just as I expected. "You have your main product, but you can diversify even if you don't have another kind of product to push."

"What do you mean?" I ask him.

I know it's just as I imagined it would be post-sex, but I can't help not feeling hurt by the nonchalance. The fact that he's back talking business as if nothing ever happened.

"I'm sure you've seen the local brewers making T-shirts and other merchandise with their logo and stuff. That's one avenue you could go toward. The other would be offering tours here. Especially during tapping season," he says.

"It's too busy during tapping season," I snap at him.

"Well, the rest of the year, then. But if I were you, I'd hire someone to do the tours for you, otherwise you'll be stuck here trying to juggle everything. And then there are packages," he continues, as if I didn't just snap at him.

What is wrong with this man?

"You could make gift sets. Maybe a cocktail we could come

up with and make kits to sell at the market or get stocked in shops. And actually, going around to bars and restaurants with cocktail and serving recipes might help a mile with their incentive to sell your product. As would be finding incentives for managers and staff. There could be a prize for the best-selling site, maybe gift vouchers. Those tend to go over well with bartenders," he continues.

Yes, the subject's interesting, and I've never thought of these things, even though I've seen lots of producers do similar, but I'm just too pissed to discuss any of this with him.

"But, of course, it all starts with confidence," he says.

"I have confidence," I snap again.

"You've got a fantastic product, a great brand, and something unique. You need to go in and act like it's the best thing since sliced bread," he says with a pointed brow.

"Okay, fine, I don't have that much confidence." I sink back in my seat, and Logan purses his lips.

"Don't do that. Don't make yourself smaller because you're not perfect or because you haven't thought of these things before," he says. "You grew up with your grandad, he taught you everything, and he supplied maple syrup to other producers. Of course he wouldn't know these things, and it was a different time then. You're doing great. You've come such a long way in the last two weeks. You've taken huge leaps of faith that even big brands are terrified of making."

"Yeah, I took some huge leaps, all right," I say without meaning to do so aloud.

"See? Exactly. And I bet it was scary, but it paid off on Saturday, didn't it? When was the last time you sold out?" he says after a pause.

I straighten up in my chair and glare back at him.

"Are you seriously going to ignore what happened between us on Saturday night?" I ask him.

I've had enough business talk and pretending.

Logan flinches and sits back.

"I'm not ignoring it," he says.

"So the fact that you came back and jumped straight into work and continued talking about work when I literally just threw a bone at you, isn't ignoring it? Wow. I don't know what to say." My voice has grown progressively louder as I've gone on.

"Says you. You're acting like nothing happened. You're the one who's gone back into being a grump with me just like you were when we first met," Logan snaps back.

It takes me by surprise. His apparent frustration. I haven't seen him get upset or angry before. It does something to my insides. He looks gorgeous and hot when he's smiling, but something about the frown and the tension in his face gets me all riled up.

"I'm just doing what you expect me to do!" I shout at him.

"Oh yeah? And what is that?" he shouts back.

And now my dick is hard. Great.

"Treating it like just sex so you're free to move on to the next hole!"

"I don't want to move on to the next hole!" he yells back and shoots up, banging his hand on the desktop.

"What *do* you want then?" I say and stand up to bang my hand too.

"You, for fuck's sake. I want you!"

The passionate rage with which he spits out the words rips me apart, but the meaning of his words puts me back together.

He just said he wants me, didn't he?

"There. Was that so hard?" I say, and that's all it takes for him to reach across the table, grab me by my shirt, and pull me into his mouth.

He attacks my lips, my tongue, my everything with fury,

and I reciprocate. It's not long before Logan climbs onto the desk and slides across until he's kneeling on it, and I have to stretch my head back in order to kiss him, his hands gripping my hair, like he's my master and I'm his servant.

"I want you. Now," he growls, and my only response is the moan that trembles out of me.

He pulls away from our kiss and looks around us at my desk. Before I can ask what he's looking for, he pushes everything off.

The paperwork, the pens, the stapler. Hell, even the bottle of maple wine that's always there. It smashes on the floor and wets the papers, but do I care?

Fuck no.

Because Logan pulls me back to him and hoists me up on the desk, until he's lying on his back with me on top of him.

One hand pins me to his mouth, the other pushes my jeans off until my ass is exposed. He cups my butt cheek and squeezes until I'm moaning again. I buck my hips so I can unbutton his pants between us and release his throbbing dick. I stroke him, massage his balls, slide my hand to his taint, and all the way to his rim, pressing my middle finger against his tight muscle.

Logan gasps in my mouth, but his cheeks ball up from his smile. He moves his hand from my butt to my hole and slips a finger in me. It only stings for a moment, but the pleasure of his finger padding at my rim more than makes up for any pain.

We finger away, lips puffy from all the kissing, but I need more. So much more.

I slither down to his crotch and swallow his cock without a second thought. Logan twitches at the move and it makes him harder in my mouth.

Logan Graves is all about girth *and* length, but I still try to take all of him in. I suck and suck, but I don't want him coming before he's had the chance to fuck me. Not now. Not today. Any other day, I would take my time to have him come undone in my mouth. What I need now is him inside me.

And since we have no lube here, good old-fashioned spit and precum will have to do.

I slip out of my pants and sit back on him, reuniting our mouths as I press his cock in my ass.

"It's going to hurt," he mumbles against my lips.

"Don't care," I tell him, and I tighten my grip around his base until his crown breaks through my muscle, taking my breath away.

I touch his forehead with mine as I try to catch my breath, and then look at him and nod. He pushes gently inside me until he rubs along my prostate and keeps on going.

"Are you okay, baby?" he asks me, stroking my temple and staring into my eyes.

"Ye-ahhh," I groan.

It's the only thing I can vocalize when he's so full inside me, when his eyes are so shiny and staring at me, when he's holding my waist as if I mean the world to him. And when he checks on me every step of the way, making sure I'm okay, until he spills inside me.

I only catch my breath for a moment before I start pumping my dick and he pulls up his shirt to catch my cum on his pink hairy skin.

"God, you're amazing," he says, cupping my face.

He uses his free hand and runs his fingers across his stomach, then brings them up to his mouth, and lets my cum drip into his mouth. He licks his fingers, eyes still on me. He looks sensational eating my seed like it's the nectar he's been craving all his life. Like it's the sap that gives him life. And I can't help it when I lean down and kiss his cum-stained lips until we're revved and ready to start round two. Only this time, we get to admire each other's cocks a lot longer than before.

We've used our shirts to wipe ourselves and are standing butt-naked in the distillery when my phone rings.

I search for my phone and find it on the floor, atop the puddle of maple wine that's started to dry out around the edges

"Um…" I say, grabbing it by the very edge and lifting it in front of Logan.

"Oops. I'll get you a new one. ASAP," he says with an apologetic, adorable pout.

"I know you will," I say, kissing him. "But how on Earth is it still working?"

He shrugs, and I use my other hand to answer the phone and put it on speaker.

"Honey, what took you so long?" Mom's voice echoes around the distillery.

"I-I was busy, Mom," I tell her, sneaking a glance at the naked mountain in front of me and his flaccid cock that still looks ginormous and so damn lickable.

"Oh, are you by any chance busy with your new boyfriend?" she asks.

Logan chokes up a laugh, and I have a hard time containing mine too.

"No comment. Did you need anything?" I ask her.

"Well, I won't take too much of your time so you can go back to your…um…business, but we'd love to have Logan and you for dinner tonight if you'd like," she says. "He's such a great gu—"

"Okay, Mom," I interrupt her. "I'll ask him and let you know."

"Okay. And ask him if he has any allergies," she says, and Logan shakes his head.

"No allergies, Mom. Talk to you later," I say and hang up on her then drop the phone on the sweat-stained desk.

"Sorry about that," I tell him.

"What for?" he asks as he starts putting his underwear and pants back on, which should be a crime against nature.

A dick like that deserves infinite airtime.

"She's getting attached to you," I say.

"Is that a bad thing?" he asks.

I shrug.

"Well, I know you don't do serious," I tell him.

"Do you now? What if I want to?"

"Want what?"

"You. Full-time," he replies.

"I'm not a job," I tell him, and he grimaces, pursing his lips to one side. "Oh, shut up."

"I mean it, though," he says.

"No, you don't."

"Stop telling me what I mean and what I don't. You think you know me so well, don't you?"

I'm feeling very naked all of a sudden, even though Logan is still topless. Things are good when we're fucking. Why can't we just keep fucking instead of making things harder than they have to be?

"Well, I know what you do. What you write. And you told me so too. The night we got drunk," I tell him.

"Oh, and because I write porn you think I can't want you? Also, did you forget what else I told you that night? The fact that it doesn't feel good anymore, that it doesn't feel special?"

"Of course I remember. That's why I know this is just another adventure for you. It's fine. I don't mind. I've accepted it."

Am I shouting again?

"You've *accepted* it? You're not an adventure, Brody. You're a destination," he says, and I really want to tell him to stop.

People shouldn't say romantic things like that if they don't mean them.

"Oh, please. Why would I be a destination?"

Logan huffs and shakes his head.

"Because you're bloody special for fuck's sake. Why can't you get it in your head that I could like you for more than just sex," he says.

"Me? Special? Pfft, there's nothing special about me." I shrug him off.

"Well…" Logan says and comes to stand right in front of me, his hand finding solace at the side of my face. "I beg to differ."

I look up at him and feel so small, yet it doesn't scare me anymore.

"Really?" I mumble.

"Really," he replies. "The most special. You're the person I'm in love with."

I take a deep breath and my lip trembles.

"Oh, that's good. Because I think I'm in love with you too."

"So good," Logan whispers as he leans into my lips and kisses me again.

And then I wake up.

Or I should. Because what are the chances this is all real? That this is happening to me?

And yet it is. It's not a dream.

This is real.

19

LOGAN

"No! Do not commit that atrocity," I yell at Brody on Friday morning.

He pauses mid-squeeze and turns to me.

"You don't like mustard?" he asks.

I snatch the yellow bottle out of his hands and throw it in the bin.

"Oh, I like mustard. English mustard. Not that American tasteless paste you guys call mustard," I tell him and remove as much of the yellow muck from my sandwich as possible.

"Um, excuse me? Tasteless paste? And what exactly is so special about your English mustard, your Highness?" he shouts, walking to the bin and taking the mustard bottle out.

"It's got definition, texture, kick."

"You're just a snob."

"If having tastebuds makes me a snob, then fine, I'm a snob."

"Tastebuds? You want to talk taste? You guys wouldn't even know what taste was if it weren't for all the Indians you colonized," he says, fire in his eyes.

I love that fire in him. He's had it all week since we had sex in the distillery. He had it during dinner with his parents. And every second since. In bed and out.

"Fair enough. British cuisine is bland. It doesn't mean we don't have taste, though," I tell him.

Brody wraps the sandwiches we've prepared for our road trip and puts his hands up.

"Okay, Mister That's-Too-Much-Butter," he says.

"Hey! I'm just trying to keep you from having a heart attack. Excuse me."

He smiles and comes over to drape his hands around my neck and kiss me.

"You are excused."

"I have to say, I'm enjoying our little arguments," I tell him.

"Well, it's certainly a new development in our relationship," he replies and lets go. "Not that I'm saying we're in a relationship. I mean relationship as in from when we started hanging out, knowing each other sort of relationship."

The fire is replaced by panic and it makes the craving to hold him and reassure him so strong it suffocates me.

"I like that," I tell him. "And no. It doesn't scare me. You don't need to worry about me. If I feel we're going too fast, I'll tell you."

"Good. I don't want any secrets or insecurities to get in the way," he says. "And I'm saying that for me as well because I'm still struggling with the whole trust issue."

And just like that I remember the bet. A pang of guilt beats my chest with a massive hammer.

No secrets. I don't want to keep secrets from him. He needs to know.

"About that—" I start, not sure where to begin.

"Whatever you're about to say, do it in the car. We're going to be late, and I want to make sure we get there on time to sign up and socialize," he says, putting the sandwiches in a bag.

"You? Want to socialize?" I ask, following him outside.

"Well, I've got to check out the competition, baby. So I'll put up with the small talk and the fake smiles," he says, and I roll my eyes at him.

We get into his pickup, already loaded with all the merchandise we're taking with us, and we set off for Dover and the much-anticipated festival.

I try to find the guts to tell him, and I even open my mouth several times to spill out the truth, but the words won't come out. I'm a coward. I know I am. But I've never had anyone like Brody in my life. I can't lose him.

Which is stupid because the closer to Dover we get, the closer to the truth we get. I'm sure Theo won't have any reservations about telling Brody what he heard. And it'll be much, much worse coming from him.

"You're very quiet this morning. Do you need another coffee?" Brody asks and picks up the thermos.

"Hm? Oh, yeah. Probably," I say and take it from his hands.

"We've got another couple of hours. You need to keep me entertained, or I'll fall asleep," he says.

"Yes, sorry. What about music?"

"Music's good."

I lean toward the radio and stop.

"Wait, you're not, like, a fan of country or something, are you?"

"What's wrong with country?"

I shrug.

"Nothing. Just not my cup of tea."

"Oh, I'm sorry, your Excellency. Please, kind sir, find your cup in my radio," Brody says in an awful, mocking accent.

"I shall have you punished for even trying to do that bloody awful accent," I tell him.

"Hey," he whines.

I turn up the music and keep watching him as some pop song plays in the background.

No, he's too important to lose. I can't have Theo telling him a perverted truth and ruining what we've got.

What we have is worth preserving. I worked hard to get him. Was it for the wrong reasons? Yes, yes it was, but somewhere along the way I actually fell in love with him. And I'm not going to let fucking Theo Coggan take that away from me.

I'll just have to keep Brody away from him. Which shouldn't be that hard considering there's a stall and a festival going on keeping us and them busy.

Which means I just have to keep Brody occupied today for the social aspect of the event. Not a problem, if you ask me. There is a lot of fun to be had in public spaces. I'm sure I can think of a way or two to distract Brody.

"What are you thinking about?" he asks me another ten minutes later.

"Nothing. Just my deadline for my book. Are you tired? Do you want me to drive for a while?"

He breaks into a laugh that I take as my answer. I don't mind. The sound of his laugh, his voice, hell even the sound of his cough is music to my ears.

When we get to Dover we check into the nearby hotel, and even though I try to lure him into a round of bumping uglies, Brody is eager to get out and sign-in on the event.

I go with him, of course. I go everywhere with him, and by the time the producers' meet and greet starts, I relax. Theo is nowhere to be seen and neither is his boyfriend.

Maybe he was lying about coming here. Maybe they won't even be here.

Relief washes all over me, and for the first time today, I let go and enjoy my time with Brody. No one is taking him away from me.

But, of course, all good things come to an end.

Theo and Skyler are there the next morning, at their own stall. And Theo won't stop staring at me from across the exhibition center.

I try to distract myself with the customers, although Brody is handling them great by himself.

He really has come a long way from the big grump I first met. And people are buying his bottles and our little mapletini cocktail kits we made earlier this week. But I can't enjoy any of it.

It all feels like a ticking timebomb.

And my time is up.

BRODY

I can't believe I didn't even want to come to the festival. It's probably the best thing I could have done for my business. Which only goes to show how much Logan has helped me find my true purpose and figure out what I want.

I want to have a successful small business. And I've already made so much profit over the last week alone. More than I ever have before. If this keeps going, I won't need to dig into Grandad's savings anymore.

But more than anything, I want Logan.

I didn't think I'd be ready for a new relationship so soon after Theo, but it turns out Logan was just the kind of medicine I needed. He's all I've ever dreamed of and so much more.

"This is excellent," says a guy standing at my stall after taking a sip of my wine. "Now, tell me, young man, how is this made?"

I thank him with a smile and walk around the stall to explain the process to him. It's only midday, but I've already gone through this a hundred times. I've recited the same thing so many times, my words start to sound like incompehensible noises. But hey, this is a festival of wine connoisseurs, so what else would I expect from the attendees.

"That's excellent. I have tried maple wine before, but I don't think I've ever had something so refined as...Brody's Secret," he says, pausing to read the label for a second.

"Thank you so much," I tell him.

"I'll make sure to buy a few bottles before the festival is over," he says, and then walks away, which is when I notice a clipboard in his hands.

"Who was that? Why was he carrying a clipboard? What's he writing now?" I ask in Logan's direction, but he doesn't answer me. "Hey, are you okay?"

I turn to look at him, but he's looking away, somewhere far off. He was acting weird all day yesterday, and he's still a little... off. As if his mind is only half here and half on something else.

"Is everything okay?" I ask him and move to drape my arms around him.

"Huh? Yes, of course," he says and reciprocates the hug.

"I can't believe how well it's going. We're almost sold out of the cocktail kits and half the bottles are gone. I could *so* get used to this."

Logan kisses my nose and smiles.

"You deserve it. All of it."

I tighten my arms around him and hold him closer to me. I'd have nothing without him. It's all thanks to him. And I make sure to tell him that.

"I only helped bring out the real you, sweetheart," he says. "That's all."

"I'm pretty sure you did far more than that," I tell him, but he's already looking at something behind me.

I probably have a customer, so I pull away half-heartedly and find Theo standing at my stall.

"What are you doing here?" Logan asks him.

Theo smirks and slides a hand across the table.

"I'm just browsing. You've changed...everything," Theo says.

"Yeah, well, it was time for a major spring-clean in my life," I tell him, pointedly.

"It's good. Maybe a bit rushed, but it's good, I guess." He goes on as if he didn't hear me, and I completely pull away from Logan to go and stand in front of him. Maybe if I do, he'll get the message he's not welcome.

"Rushed? I'd say it was way overdue."

"Maybe. Maybe," Theo says and picks up a bottle, fingers tracing the new label. "Brody's Secret, huh? I guess everyone's got secrets around here nowadays, don't they?"

"What is that supposed to mean?" I ask him, feeling the tightness on my face. I know we came here to make him jealous and show him I've moved on, but gee, after everything that happened with Logan, I don't care about Theo anymore. Not an inch.

"Why don't you go back to your boyfriend? You're not welcome here," Logan snarls at him.

A few people walk past the stall and stare at the heated conversation.

"Why? This is a public space. You can't tell me where to be," Theo says and laughs. "Can you believe this guy? The cheek of him after what he did." Theo turns to me and shakes his head, pointing at Logan.

"What are you talking about?" I ask him, crossing my arms.

Logan stiffens beside me, and Theo smiles. He looks so creepy.

"I can't believe I never noticed how creepy your smile is."

"Hey, I'm creepy? What about your 'boyfriend?' He's creep-central if you ask me."

"Well, we aren't," Logan says.

"Creep-central? What the hell are you talking about? Are you drunk?"

Theo looks at Logan and tilts his head to the side, the amusement still apparent on his face.

"Oh. He doesn't know, does he?"

"Know what?" I ask Theo, but he starts laughing instead of answering. I turn to Logan.

His face is dark, and his shoulders are hunched.

"What is going on? What's happening? Logan?"

"Your 'boyfriend' made a bet with that guy from Vino and Veritas that he could get you into bed. You didn't know that?" he says and turns to Logan. "Wait, are you still trying to get him into bed? Really? He didn't waste any time with me. First date and, bam, we're fucking."

Logan launches at Theo and grabs him by the collar.

"Shut your bloody mouth before I do it for you," Logan growls.

And now a lot more people are watching.

"Oh yeah? I'd love to see you try."

Logan raises a fist, about to strike. And boy, I'd love to see that happen, but...

"Is it true?" I ask.

He must have heard me because he pauses, but he doesn't turn to look at me.

"Logan... Is. It. True?" I repeat.

"Of course it's true. I heard them talking about—" Theo starts, but Logan pushes him off, and Theo stumbles, landing on the ground.

Logan turns and tries to take hold of my hands, but I have to take a step back.

"Brody…it's not what it sounds like. It's not like that at all," he says.

His eyes speak the truth. He can barely stand to look at me. His whole face is red. He's guilty as they come, no matter what he's trying to tell me.

And I'm the fucking fool that fell for his charms.

"So everything was a lie, huh?" I snap and take another step back.

"No, Brody. It wasn't a lie. Nothing was a lie—"

He tries to touch me, to kiss me. I don't know what the fuck he's trying to do, but I can't stand the sight of him, let alone his touch.

I knew I should have trusted my gut. Logan Graves was always bad news; I just refused to see it. I let him into my life, and he only came to crash it.

"What did you win? Huh? What was the prize for sleeping with me?" I shouted at him.

"Oh, so you did fuck—" Theo laughs from the floor.

"You can shut up. No one's talking to you, you pathetic little man."

"I'm sorry for trying to help," he says.

"You're not trying to help. You're trying to hurt me. You're trying to make yourself feel better, bigger than me. As if hurting me once wasn't enough. You just want to keep hitting the weak punching bag, don't you? You're a sad excuse of a man, and I can't believe I didn't see it before I said yes."

I can barely contain myself. There's rage inside me. So much rage. So much pain. So much of everything, I'm about to explode.

"Sheesh? I'm pathetic? Have you looked at yourself in the mirror, Brody? You're a sad man, so attached to your grandad's pathetic little business that you can't even see what a failure you are—"

"You have done enough. Get the fuck out of here." Logan grabs him by the collar again and lifts him to his feet. "Piss off," he shouts and pushes Theo away.

Theo resists, but then he walks off, backward, watching me, taking pleasure in his work.

God! What did I ever see in that man?

"Brody." Logan turns around again, but whatever he's about to say, whatever half-baked lie, I don't want to hear it.

"So? What was it? What did you win? What was I *worth*?"

"It was nothing, Brody. The bet doesn't mean anything to me. It was—"

"Oh, so it was all for nothing. I was just a game? Just something to mess around with in Vermont until you go off to your next destination?"

"You're painting me as if I'm an evil man," he says.

"And? Aren't you? Didn't you decide to insert yourself into my life and toy with my pain? What *does* that make you? A saint?"

"Brody—" He tries to touch me again, but I don't know what I'll do if he succeeds.

So I step behind the counter and grab my keys.

"Don't!" I tell him. "You wanna get paid for your bet? Here!" I throw all the cash that I've made so far at him.

Dramatic. I know. It's probably quite the show for all the attendees to watch, but I can't think straight. My mind has jumped ship.

"Here. Have it. Have it all. It was all your idea anyway. I'm going."

I turn and run as far and as fast as possible. I need to get out of here. I need to get him out of my life and put as much distance between us as I physically can.

I exit the exhibition center and find my pickup in the parking lot.

As I drive away from the festival, I see Logan in my rearview mirror staring at me speeding off.

"Good. He can kiss my ass goodbye," I tell myself, and keep going until he's a dot and then continue further.

It's only when I'm far away enough that I let the tears I've been holding in fall.

"I'm an idiot. A big-ass idiot," I keep telling myself all the way back.

By the time I get home, it's dark outside and the tears have long since dried, but my determination hasn't vanished.

I grab a suitcase, pack everything I can fit in it, and drive to my parents.

21

LOGAN

He's gone.

I can't believe he's gone.

I can't believe I didn't get a chance to explain. To show him what he means to me.

My worst fear has come to life. Of course it has. Why wouldn't it? I'm a horrible man. I deserve all of it.

But that doesn't mean there isn't someone else that needs to pay.

"Hey, wanker!" I shout when I go up to the maple syrup stand Theo is at.

As he turns around, my knuckles connect with his face and he stumbles backwards.

"That's for letting go of such an amazing guy," I say, and as he tries to stand straight again, I punch him once more. "And that's for pushing him away from me."

"Oh my God, Theo!" Skyler yelps and comes to Theo's aid. "Are you out of your mind?" he shouts at me.

"Yes," I snap. "If it weren't for your stupid boyfriend here, I'd still have Brody in my life. But no. He can't stand the fact that he found someone who actually loves and cares for him.

It doesn't matter that he didn't want to do it himself, he doesn't want anyone else to have him. Isn't that right? Wanker?"

Theo moves his jaw from side to side, cringing, his dark brows creasing as he glares back at me.

"What did you do?" Skyler asks him.

"Just told Brody the truth—ouch," Theo says and presses his cheek.

"What truth? What does it have to do with you?" Skyler asks.

"Nothing. It's got nothing to do with him. He just thinks he knows what he heard when, in fact, he just wanted to prove a point, didn't you? To dig the knife a little deeper?" I tell the young man.

"I thought you said you were over him," Skyler says.

"I am," Theo says.

"Oh really? Is that why you came to the farm a few weeks ago after you saw us together? You thought you were going to get him alone, didn't you? And maybe you'd convince him to suck your dick again or something?"

"Shut up. That's not true," Theo says.

"Then why do you care? Why do you care so much about Brody?" I ask him.

Theo looks from me to Skyler and back, flinching at the already bruised cheek. I don't do violence, but boy it feels good seeing the arrogant man in pain. Especially after the damage he's caused.

"Because I do. I spent two years of my life with him. He's a great guy and deserves better."

"Then why did you walk out on him? If he's such a great guy? Huh?"

"Fuck off. I don't owe you an explanation," Theo answers.

"You owe me one, though," Skyler says.

"Babe. Don't listen to him. He's a player. He's just pissed that he got caught in the game."

"And I repeat, why do you care? Why do you have to get involved?"

"Because he was hurting him. Playing with his feelings. Did you know he bet he could get him into bed? That's why he got close to him. To win a bet."

Every word that comes out of Theo's mouth makes me want to punch him again. But he's not worth it. He's not worth my fists, my freedom, or my attention. He's a worthless piece of shit.

And so am I. Because he's right, of course. I am a player. I played with Brody's feelings. It doesn't matter that I caught them too. I should have come clean to him. I had so many opportunities. Yet I decided keeping Brody close to me was better than telling him the truth and letting him decide if he still wanted me.

Maybe things would be better if I'd told him myself. If I had explained what happened. But that chance is gone.

"Yes, but I fell in love with him, for fuck's sake. That's what you don't get. It doesn't matter if I won the bet or not. I was ready to change my life for him. To commit myself to him. But you went and ruined it."

I don't know if I'm saying it to Theo or myself, but as soon as I finish, I deflate. I can't do this anymore. I can't waste my time on this puny man. I need to go. I need to get to Brody.

"Yeah, right," Theo chuckles. "Can you believe this man?"

Skyler shakes his head.

"Yes. But I can't believe you," he says.

Theo is taken aback and stares at Skyler.

"What are you saying?"

"What are we doing, Theo? Where are we going? Why are you with me?"

"Because I like you," Theo answers.

"But you're still in love with Brody. You're obviously still hung up on him, aren't you? Otherwise, why would you stoop so low?" Skyler asks him, and Theo stumbles backward until he leans against the stall.

"I was trying to open his eyes."

"Really? And did you allow this man to explain himself? Did you allow him to tell his version? Or did you twist everything so you can split them up?"

"I just told him the truth."

"No, you didn't. You heard me talking to Oz. You heard the warning he gave me. And you heard me admit that I'm in love with him, but you left that out of your revelation, didn't you?"

"Well…it was loud at the bookshop. They've got that music playing in the background. I didn't hear everything."

"Oh. My. God," Skyler exclaims. "I cannot believe you. You're such a liar. You're pathetic."

"But, baby—" Theo tries to step closer to his boyfriend, but Skyler raises his hands to block him.

"No. I don't want to be with someone so toxic," Skyler says. "I can't believe I didn't see it sooner."

Theo's eyes darken even more, and he huffs.

"Toxic? Me? Huh! And what about you? You think you're a ray of fucking sunshine?" Theo shouts.

"Adorable," Skyler mutters.

"Yeah, whatever. Good luck finding someone who'll be happy coming second to cows and fucking trees! You sad fuck," Theo shouts at Skyler and walks off.

"Wanker," I yell after him.

"Asshole," Skyler says at the same time.

We stand opposite each other for a few awkward moments, until Skyler leans back against his stall and stares.

"Did you really bet on a guy?" he asks.

"Yeah." I sigh.

Why does it matter anymore? It's the truth anyway.

"And you really fell in love with him?"

"Yes."

"And have you had the chance to tell him?"

I shake my head, taking a deep breath when I'm done.

"I'm stuck here," I say.

"No, you're not. I can drive you back."

I blink several times, waiting for him to laugh or mock me, but he doesn't.

"Do you mean that?"

"Sure. But you have to promise you actually love him," he says.

"More than anything I've ever loved in the world," I say, and Skyler smiles.

"Then you better pack up, tiger. Because we've got a long way to go to win your man back."

"Thank you. Thank you so much," I tell him and run off to Brody's stall.

There's a man there, holding a whole stack of money in his hand and people around him picking up stray notes.

"What's going on?" I ask.

The people on their knees look up at me.

"We wanted to help," a woman says and hands me the money she's already collected.

In the whole frenzy with Brody, I didn't even think about the stock or all the money he threw. I just had to go after him.

But these people...they could have taken the money for themselves, yet they chose to help us.

If that isn't signature Vermont hospitality, I don't know what is.

"Thank you," I say. "Thank you so much."

I reach for the tin box and put all the notes in as more and more people hand me what they've collected.

Last is the guy with the big stack in his hands, resting on top of a clipboard.

"You're so kind," I tell him, taking the money from him.

"It's nothing," he says. "Is Mr. Mercier coming back?"

There's a strike of pain in my chest at the mention of Brody.

"I don't know," I mumble.

I hope he does. I hope he listens. That he believes me. But…

"Well, you work with him, don't you?" the man asks.

"Um…yeah, I am. I do," I say and set the box on the table. "Why? Is there something wrong?"

"No, no. Nothing wrong. I… I'm John Miles, and I'm part of the festival committee," he says.

"Nice to meet you, Mr. Miles."

"Please, just call me John. My colleagues and I have been going around tasting all the products today, and I'm happy to announce that Brody's Secret Maple Wine is our chosen winner for Innovative Product of the Year," he says.

"Really? That's fantastic. I didn't even realize you guys were going around tasting everything," I say.

"Oh, yes. We're always around getting tipsy on all the amazing products from around the state."

He laughs and looks at a camera guy, inviting him over, and it's then I notice a girl standing behind the judge, holding a little star-shaped award.

"A picture for our website?" he asks, and I hesitantly let them, even though I've got nothing to do with the wine.

This is all Brody's hard work. He needs to be here. He should be the one accepting the award and all the praise. Not me. Definitely not me.

But this is too good an opportunity for him, and I want to at least give him the award.

When we're done with pictures, the guy buys a box of wine from me, and I help him carry it to his van.

Naturally, when I'm back, the stall is crammed with people, so I have no choice but to sell more wine to them, which delays my setting off, but at least it gets rid of most of the stock.

All I have left to pack an hour later are two boxes of wine and all the display items.

I move everything to Skyler's stall and help him move both our stuff to his pickup before we drive off back home.

"You're really kind to do this for me," I tell him on the way.

"It's not a big deal," he says.

"I beg to differ, but never mind. How are you feeling? I'm sorry about Theo."

Skyler glances at me and shrugs.

"It's not your fault. It's mine for not seeing what a jerk he is. But I guess I was too busy with my *cows and trees* to notice."

"I'm sure that man can't utter a truth even if his life depended on it. I wouldn't worry about it," I say.

Skyler shrugs and checks his wing mirror.

"Oh no. He's probably right. I spend most of my time on my farm. Which is probably why my dating record includes a man who thinks being part of pyramid schemes will make him a millionaire," he says.

"No way. Really? People still fall for that shit?"

"I don't know about people, but *Theo* certainly does." Skyler laughs.

I laugh too. It's not really that funny, but if I don't laugh I might just cry, and I can't handle that. Not right now. I can't let go. Because I'll be a mess, and good luck winning Brody back then.

Something in the car snarls and Skyler bites his lips.

"Sorry. I think that's my body telling me it needs food. Stat. Are you hungry?"

I nod, so we make a stop at a fast-food drive-thru and eat in the car before we continue our journey.

He drops me off at Brody's farm where my car is still parked and helps me unpack everything and put it in the distillery.

"You're a lot like Brody, you know? You two would get along, I think," I tell Skyler when he's back behind his wheels.

"How about you try to win him back, and if he doesn't take you, I'll give it a try." He winks at me.

"Hey! I meant as friends. Don't get all cheeky now." I warn him, but he laughs and drives off.

When he's out of view, I look at the house. All the lights are off. And his car isn't here. Is he still on the way? Did something happen to him? Or did he run off somewhere he knows I can't find him.

"Where are you, Brody? Where are you? This can't be the end."

BRODY

"Sweetie, what's up?"

"Nothing," I tell Mom for the hundredth time.

"So why are you staying here?" she asks as I change the TV channel yet again.

Is there nothing to watch on cable anymore? Why are all the channels showing crap?

"Why? You're the one who keeps begging me to come by more often? I thought you'd be happy to have me to yourself for a few days."

Mom looks from the TV set to me. She pierces me with her gaze, as if that's gonna make me tell her all my secrets, so when it doesn't work, she huffs.

I press the channel button on the remote and the TV blinks through all the different networks until it's nothing but a blur.

"Stop that," she says and snatches the remote from my hands. "What happened?"

"Mom!" I raise my voice.

"Why aren't you in Dover?"

"It was boring."

"But, you could have sold some more bottles—"

"I sold out."

"That's excellent. You could have stayed—"

"Didn't want to."

"What about Logan?"

I bite down on the inside of my cheeks so hard, I think I taste blood.

"Don't ever say that name again," I snarl under my breath.

Mom puts her hand on my shoulder and sighs.

"What did he do?"

Hmm…where do I start? From his conniving game? His dirty flirtations with a hidden purpose? Hiding the truth of his motives? Betting on me as if I were a horse and not a human being?

There is a whole galore of deceptions and heartbreak that I have neither the energy nor the mental capacity to unpack.

I was a fool to let this man into my life. And an even bigger fool to trust him with anything more than a conversation.

"I don't want to talk about it," I say.

"You guys looked so happy together. I haven't seen you smile like when you're with him for a long while. I'm sure whatever happened, you two will—"

"Mom, please stop," I plead with her.

I can feel the threat of another stream of tears coming through, and I bite the inside of my cheek harder.

I will *not* cry for this man. He doesn't deserve it. He's not worth it. He doesn't deserve any more of me.

"Is there anything you want me to do?" she asks.

I shake my head, but as I do, it's like I shake my feelings out because all the tears *do* come out, and I can't stop them.

"How about we start with some hot cocoa?" Mom coos, stroking my hair affectionately before retreating to the kitchen to get started.

My mind keeps flashing back to the moments we've

shared. From his gutsy display of love at the market, when I didn't even know his name, to our intimate nights together.

I thought it was real. The person hiding underneath all that confidence. The man who was ready to settle. The guy who had never fallen in love.

How could it all be a lie? How is it possible? How can anyone fake it for so long, so well?

"Here you go, honey," Mom says when she returns with a cup in her hands.

I take it from her and look at the whipped cream and the marshmallows, feel the warmth of the cup against my hand, but it does nothing to appease the storm inside.

"Are you sure you don't want to talk? It might help," she says, taking a seat beside me.

"No, Mom. I don't think I can," I tell her and drink my hot beverage.

It's the only thing I can think of to occupy my mouth. Because I do want to talk to her. Of course I do. But I'll become another heaping mess if I do, and I just...can't. I'm not going to break down because of this man.

It's not his fault I fell in love with him so quickly, and it's not his fault I let him into my life. Yes, he had ulterior motives, but it's my fault. I let myself be duped after everything that happened to me. There's no bigger idiot than me.

"Why don't I go make your bed?" Mom says and pats my knee.

She goes off to my old room to prepare it for the night, and I allow myself to get completely lost in a TV show. Not that I follow the story or hear the dialogue. I just stare at the pretty colors and the enamored characters and, for a second, a very hot second, I forget the pain.

Eventually I go to bed and eventually I fall asleep for a few hours. Then, I spend the day either in bed or on the couch.

On one hand, it's extremely boring. I'm so used to doing something, to being in the distillery and working or being in the house cleaning or listening to an audiobook while I'm doing the laundry.

But on the other hand, there's a joy in doing nothing after years and years of hard work and no play.

So Sunday comes and goes, as does Monday and Tuesday, and by Wednesday, I may not feel any better, but I really need to go back home and get the barrels rolled. The last thing I need right now is for the casks to dry out and start leaking.

I'm all for going alone, but Dad won't let me, so he tags along and helps me with all the stuff I need to do around the distillery. I do find two boxes of wine stacked at the entrance as well as all the display stuff from the festival, which means Logan has been here. However, I still don't turn my phone on. Who needs a cell anyway? I can check the time on my watch. I'm staying with my parents for now, so I don't need to call them. And it's not like I have the biggest social life on the planet, so no one will miss me.

I know eventually I'll have to turn it on, and that I can just block Logan's number. But even the thought of finding a message or a missed call or any trace of him on my cell, terrifies me.

An hour later, I go into the kitchen to make Dad and me a snack and another round of coffee, and that's when I hear a car pull up in my driveway.

I walk up to the window and see Logan's rental. The coffee pot almost slips out of my hands.

What is he doing here?

I rush back to the distillery, hoping to lock it up before he can walk in, but it's too late.

"Brody. Please. Hear me out," he says, running to the door and putting his foot in the way so I can't shut it.

"Go away," I tell him.

He doesn't look like himself. He looks beaten and tired. There's no smile or smirk on his face. The confident man is gone.

"Good," I say.

I hope he feels like shit. I hope he never gets any sort of absolution. I hope this makes him miserable for a very long time.

"You didn't let me explain," he says.

"What is there to explain? That you used me? That you lied to me? There's nothing to explain. You're scum. And I'm an idiot because I saw who you were from the start, and yet, I still let you into my life."

Logan pulls his hand out of his pocket and places it firmly on the metal door, but he doesn't try to push it open any further.

"You're right. I am scum. The biggest scum on earth. But I still fell in love with you. And you're not an idiot. You're special. The most special man in the world," he says.

I want to believe him. To open the door and take him in my arms. Forget everything that happened.

But I can't.

Fool me once, shame on you. Fool me twice...

I won't be fooled twice by him.

"Of course I am. Until you find the next 'special' man," I say.

"No. That's not—"

"You know, I'm really busy, and I really don't have the time for you, so if you don't mind," I say and try to shut the door again.

Loga shakes his head and pushes the door wide.

"I... There's something else," he says and looks inside the distillery. "I brought all the money back from the festival."

"Keep it. Consider it payment for winning your bet," I say.

"Brody, please," he says.

I glare at him, and his chest deflates.

"I don't need it. It's yours."

"No. I insist. You won your bet fair and square. Besides, you spent how many hours helping me out? Take it as payment for services rendered."

"You're not listening to me," he shouts.

"No, you're not listening, Logan. I'm done with you. D-O-N-E, done. So take your money, take your car, and get the hell out of my life."

Logan looks at the floor, his hand dropping from the door, and he bites his bottom lip. He's never looked weaker, smaller than he does now.

After everything he's done, I love watching him crumble in front of me. He deserves it. The man with all the conquests at the pity of a regular Joe. That should teach him for his cockiness.

"I…fine. I'll go. But there's something you *should* have," he says and goes up to his car.

I watch him open the passenger door, take out my red tin box and something that I can't quite identify, and then come back to stand outside.

"You won this," he says and gives me the thing resting on top of the tin box.

It's a translucent star-shaped statue with a sign on the bottom that reads Innovative Product of the Year.

"I-I won this?" I ask him, for a moment forgetting how mad I am with him. But only for a moment.

"You did. They wanted to take a picture with you for their website, but you'd already left, so they took one with me. I'm sure if you call them you can arrange to have your picture taken instead," he says.

I can't believe I won an award. This is…this is great. This is all I've ever dreamed of, and I can't even celebrate because of this fucking asshole standing in front of me.

"Thanks," I snap and make another attempt to shut the door on him.

He stops me again and hands me the tin box.

"I can't keep it. Take it. Please," he says.

"If I take it, will you promise to leave me the hell alone?"

He stares at me for moments, moments that make me want to forget everything again and take him back.

But yet again, that would be a mistake.

I'm not a toy to be played with. I'm not a person to be used and abused as someone else sees fit. I'm my own damn man, and I won't take any more of this shit.

He's like Theo. That's what I have to remind myself. He's an arrogant piece of shit. Only, he chases men instead of money.

"If that will make you happy," he says.

"It will," I tell him and take the box from him. "Now go. And don't come back."

Logan stands there as I finally close the door on him, and I'm ready to move on with my life.

It won't be easy, but I'm ready.

I just have to see it as it is. Even though he broke my heart, he gave me something great. He taught me how to sell Grandad's wine. And that's exactly what I'll do.

It wasn't all for nothing. Even if I lost my heart to Logan, it wasn't all for nothing.

LOGAN

Life without Brody is…

It's empty. But then again, my life hasn't been full for a long while. As much as I try to hide or deny it; I haven't been happy in years.

Which is why his loss hurts so much more. Because he's the one and only person who ever clawed themselves into my heart whether I liked it or not.

And I could have made him happy. I know I could.

But there's no way I can prove my love for him. Not after what I've done. Not after what Theo did to him.

And so I have to let him go and be happy without me. If you love someone, let them go. Isn't that what they say? Isn't that the least selfish thing to do?

It's the least I can do after intruding in his life and taking a seat where I wasn't welcome. So that's what I do. I let him go.

My only consolation is my writing. Despite everything, I find escape in the book he birthed. Happily ever after might not be a real thing, but at least in my book it's achievable. And I think that's why I'm not able to stop writing it. And why I finish it in record time. And even though I'm done, I start another one. A different couple, a different story, but same feelings. I just want to give someone else, even if they're fictional, the chance to find true happiness. Like I did. Even if I let it slip from my fingers. My fault, of course.

"Hello." I pick up my phone when it rings and look outside my window.

The sky is gray like my head, the trees barren, and the roads full of orange and brown leaves blowing in the wind.

"Hey, sweetheart. You all right?" Chloe's voice chimes in my ear.

"I'm fine," I tell her.

"Are you back in London now?"

"Yeah. I arrived on Sunday," I say.

It's been ten days since I last saw Brody. I would have stayed in Vermont. I'd have kept the flat there longer. Lorelai was more than happy to extend my dates, but everything reminded me of him. And without him, I couldn't just stay there and think about how lonely my life is.

I'd rather be lonely at home. Or whatever this place is.

"Well, welcome back, then. Listen, honey! I read the book," she says.

"Already? I only sent it yesterday."

"Well, what can I say? Once I started, I couldn't stop."

I get off my desk chair and pace around the room, wondering if I want to know what she thought.

"And?" I say when the pause has gone on long enough.

"You were right. It's not your usual thing," she says.

"I know. I'm sorry. It's crap, isn't it? I'll start again. Don't send it to Janet yet. I'll write something else and—"

"Logan, honey, it was great. What are you on about?" she says.

"What are *you* on about?"

"Your book. *Falling for the Sugarmaker*," she says.

"Well, yeah. But you said it's different."

"I didn't mean *bad* different. I meant *good* different. It's so sweet and cute. I don't think you've ever written cute before. I think this is the best book you've ever written. Even if the sex scenes were too mild for my liking," she says.

I hear her. I'm just not sure how I feel about what she's saying.

For some reason, her compliments make me feel even worse than I already do. Like I'm still being a sleazeball, profiting from Brody's heartache. And mine.

Of course, the story has nothing to do with us. Yes, there's a bet involved and close proximity. But it's not our story. Not on paper anyway. On feelings and emotions, yes, it is. But only he would ever know that. If he ever reads it.

But that still doesn't make it okay somehow. It feels like I cheated my way through a book.

Whereas all my other books have sprung from real stories, it has never bothered me before. Not as much as it does now. Not as much as with this one.

"So…" Chloe says in my ear, continuing where she left off. "I know you told me to read it first before I sent it to Janet, but as soon as I read the first few chapters, I needed her to see it too. So she's finished it as well."

"Oh God. She hates it, doesn't she?" I ask, finally collapsing on my desk chair and looking at my home office. I picked everything in it carefully when I bought it. I made it the perfect escape and workplace. But now it's like a cold and empty room.

Will I ever feel happy again? Will I ever *be* happy?

"She loves it. And she's excited to put a Logan Graves romance in the market. They've been looking to diversify their romance line lately, you know, with more LGBTQ+ content, so she thinks your book could be the start of a rainbow series."

"Really? She really said that?"

"Okay, what is wrong with you? Why won't you believe anything I say?" Chloe asks.

I sigh and shrug. Why indeed.

"It's nothing. I'm sorry. Go on."

"She did have a question for you, though. She wants to know if you'll be going back to erotica for your next book or if you officially want to turn to romance?" she asks.

Do I want to go back to screwing guys and writing about my experience with them? Or even pool up ideas from my existing adventures and make them into more erotic stories?

Is that even a question? Not anymore. Not for me.

"I think I'll turn to romance," I say.

I can't even stand the idea of sleeping with anyone else other than Brody. Of being in any other man's company.

I might have won the bet, but maybe I should act like I lost it and go celibate.

Not that I can imagine having the urge to sleep with anyone in the near future. But maybe going three months without it, or even longer, will really help me feel at peace. Get over my addiction and perhaps, maybe, find happiness again.

I don't know what the future holds, but I want to at least try.

"I've already started another one," I say.

I wasn't planning on telling her, but after the news— exciting news, even, though I don't feel excited—I want to tell her.

I spent so much time stuck and uninspired. It's like loving Brody has opened up this part of me, this part that wants all the cozy, good, fuzzy stuff I told myself I never wanted, and I don't ever want to stop writing.

At least putting them down into words helps me live vicariously through the men I come up with. Even if those men look extremely like Brody.

And probably will for a long time to come.

Even if I never see him again, his memory will be forever etched into my mind.

And I may have won my bet, but I lost my heart...

To him.

24

10 MONTHS LATER

BRODY

When I make my way back home on Monday morning, with yet another award under my belt, I'm going through all the ways I can put the accolades I've garnered over the last ten months on both my website and my bottles.

Since the Harvest Festival, demand has been crazy. So much so that I had to increase the unit price on my bottles and my cocktail kits.

I've more than made Grandad's savings back, so I no longer have to rely on those to run my business.

There's still a long way to go, and maple wine is still a niche product, but I don't need much to get by.

Things have never been better.

And yet, I'm still not over him.

I still look at the door every time someone visits my distillery—which is a lot more often these days—and expect to find Logan behind it. But that never happens. Why would it? I told him to get out of my life, and he obliged.

But with time, I've convinced myself that I was wrong.

That I should have listened to him. I should have believed him.

I know, of course, it's time distorting my memories, but it doesn't make things easier.

Truth is, we were never meant to be. He lied to me and used me. I never meant anything to him. Yet it's so hard to remember that when I wake up and wish he were in my bed, lying next to me, watching me sleep with those steely blue eyes and that smile that could make my insides melt.

I still stalk him on his website every now and again. Look at his author picture and how sexy he looks.

I've even read all his books. Jerked off to all of them, imagined myself in place of all his lovers. Daydreaming what it would be like if we were together and we could experience all those incredible things.

I'm hoping another year will heal those wounds and I can forget him. If only I could stop myself from going on his website.

On my way to the house, I stop at the postbox and pick up the mail. There's a small but heavy package with no return address, so I don't know who it's from.

I drive to the house, and once I turn off the engine, I rip through the envelope.

As I thought, it's a book. There's a stunning guy on the cover, short curly hair, big hazel eyes, topless, and looking right at me.

But I don't care about him. My eyes focus on the title and name on the bottom.

Insatiable by Logan Graves.

He sent me his book? Why? Why send me this when he's not attempted any other form of communication in ten months?

I open the first few pages and there it is.

A dedication.

For Brody

And a handwritten note.

I'm sorry. Yours, forever.

I can't stop reading the last two words. I read them over and over again and my heart does all sorts of somersaults at the mere suggestion.

What is wrong with me? Why do I care so much? What is there to care about?

I leave everything in the car and head straight for the house. I was planning on getting straight to work as soon as I returned, but I can't control the urge to read this book.

I'm addicted to his written escapades. Even with my heavy dislike for the guy, I don't seem to have the ability to dislike his work, no matter how dirty it is.

It's probably the reason why I haven't felt the need to have sex with anyone since him. Because his adventures keep my hand and fingers busy.

I go to the living room, sit back and open the book to the first page.

Chapter after chapter, Logan pulls me into his story, and I find myself in so many places. I find him in all the others. The names may be different, the professions may not be exactly the same, but damn it, he's written a book about us.

How he bet on fucking the sweet, lonely sugarmaker. How said sugarmaker was the grumpiest guy in town. How the other character has never fallen in love, playing with the guys he's been with and their emotions.

I don't know why, but I can't stop myself indulging in the story, even though I know the outcome so well. Even though I can feel the imminent heartbreak. Although, how the hell would he know how I felt?

I skip lunch and snack on cheese and crackers for dinner.

There's plenty of coffee by my side as I go through the pages. But I'm done before bedtime.

I'm shocked before bedtime.

I cry before bedtime.

Because for all the fiction and the liberties, it's clear as day he's written our story. Only it's not what I thought it was.

He truly was in love with me. He didn't mean to, but he fell for me. Only, in the book, it's not the ex that tells the guy the truth. It's the guy himself.

And forgiveness? It comes straight away. There's no fight. No heartbreak. The happy ever after is inevitable.

But it's not any of these that shake me up inside.

It's the Acknowledgements.

There isn't a long list of names and gratitude.

Just one line.

What should have happened.

LOGAN

"What's your name?" I ask.

"Jen," the woman in front of me says, and I open the flap of the book and sign it to her.

She thanks me, and I smile. Another woman steps up to my table, and I take her copy in my hands.

I look behind her, at the long line of people. Mostly women, but more than a fair share of gay men waiting for me to sign their copies of *Insatiable*.

The entire Q&A is a haze, and the signing isn't going any better.

My eyes keep darting to the door, to the counter, to the windows.

It's not that I expect him to show up, but I was hoping he would. Of course, I don't know if he even received my parcel last week. And maybe he doesn't know I'm back in Burlington for a signing. Or maybe he doesn't care.

But I still hope he shows. Chloe doesn't understand why I wanted to start my tour here, but to me, it made sense.

It's like coming back to the source of the story. Where it was inspired. But also because I'm hoping I'll bump into him. Or he'll bump into me. Or that we'll still be able to have our happily ever after, ten months later.

But he's not here. And when the line goes down and the last person leaves my table, I'm ready to break down, to give up and go back to my hotel room.

"You know," someone says behind me, their voice a balm to my aching heart. "I have a bet."

I turn around just as he comes into my line of view, holding a copy of my book in his hand, and sporting an unreadable face.

Brody.

How I missed his face, the sexy eyes, his puffy lips. Everything about him. His frown. His smile. His laugh.

"Wh-what?" I ask when he stands at my table, holding my book with both hands in front of his crotch.

"I said, I made a bet with myself."

I'm not entirely sure I will like his answer. And I don't know if I'm prepared for a scene if that's what he's here for. But the apology flies out of my mouth before I can even think about it.

"Are you not going to ask me what kind of bet I made?" he asks, ignoring me.

I swallow a knot on my throat.

"What did you bet?" I ask.

Brody moves his hands to the middle of the table and leans

forward, smoldering look and all, and whispers, "I made a bet with myself that I can get the author of this book in my bed and into my heart," he says. "Would you care to help me win it?"

I watch his lips move, but I'm not sure I understand what he says.

Did he...is he...

"Huh?"

Brody grabs my chin and leans even closer to my face, until he's only a breath away.

"I said, I bet I can spend the rest of my life with Logan Graves if he really wants me to."

Am I being pranked? I'm being pranked, right? There's cameras everywhere, and Brody is in on it, to get back at me for what I did. Right?

"Do-do you mean it?" I ask him, my voice barely a whisper between us.

Brody pulls away and stands up straight, then he walks around the table and sits on it, facing me.

"That depends," he says.

"On?"

"On whether this book is a declaration of your love for me," he replies, running a hand over my cheek.

"It is," I say.

This isn't a prank. I know what it is. It's a dream. I'm not really here. I'm not really in Burlington, Vermont, and Brody isn't really here.

I'm just having one of those million nightmares that end in heartbreak every single time.

"Then, I bet you I can spend the rest of my life with you," he says.

Oh, to hell with it. If this is a dream, it doesn't have the worst of plots. I might as well go with the flow and let the disaster strike me whenever, if it means I get to spend more time with him.

"Deal," I say and lift my hand between us.

Brody looks at it and then back at me.

"I was hoping we could seal the deal with a kiss," he says.

"Anything you want."

Brody lowers his head closer to my lips, and the moment I feel their trace on mine, I pull back.

"Wait a minute. You-you're real," I say.

Brody doesn't laugh or smile. His face relaxes, and I finally see the sadness in it.

"I am. And so are my feelings," he says. "What about yours?"

"So I'm not dreaming?" I ask.

"Is this a dream?" Brody counters and kisses me.

Our mouths reunite, our tongues reacquaint themselves with one another, and my soul finally feels at home. After so long—too long—without him.

This is real.

This is happening.

"Does that mean you forgive me?" I ask when he ends the kiss and I look back at him.

And there it is.

That smile. Creeping in from under all that sadness. That smile that changed everything for me. That changed my life.

"I think I forgave you a long time ago. I just didn't know what to do about it," he says.

"I love you, Brody. I love you so much. You're the best thing that ever happened to me. I'm so sor—"

He rests his fingers on my lips and pinches them together.

"I know. I love you, Logan. And I'm sorry I was too stubborn to let you explain. To believe you."

"You were right to be stubborn, though. I betrayed you. I lied," I say.

"That's all in the past now," he says.

"Wh-what made you change your mind?"

Brody looks at the book on the table.

"This. And Oz," he says.

"H-how?"

Brody shrugs.

"When I came in to ask about your signing, he told me what really happened."

"He did?"

Brody smiles.

"So...Mr. Graves, what do you want to do about us?"

"I want to be with you. Forever after," I say, and that seems to please him because his smile brightens, and he leans forward to kiss me again.

"Good answer," he mutters under his breath and takes hold of my jaw. "Now how about we get out of here and into my bed?"

"I thought you'd never ask," I say and stand up.

"Oh, Mr. Graves, you're insatiable," he says and squeezes my face in his hand, kissing my lips.

"Only for you."

THE
END